D0929440

Raiders of the Western & Atlantic

Other Five Star Titles by Tim Champlin:

The Last Campaign (1996)
The Survivor (1996)
Deadly Season (1997)
Swift Thunder (1998)
Lincoln's Ransom (1999)
The Tombstone Conspiracy (1999)
Wayfaring Strangers (2000)
Treasure of the Templars (2000)
A Trail to Wounded Knee (2001)
By Flare of Northern Lights (2002)

Raiders of the Western & Atlantic

A Western Story

Tim Champlin

Five Star • Waterville, Maine

Five Star First Edition Western Series.

Published in 2002 in conjunction with
Golden West Literary Agency.

Set in 11 pt. Plantin.

Printed in the United States on permanent paper.

Library of Congress Cataloging-in-Publication Data

Champlin, Tim, 1937–
Raiders of the western & Atlantic : a western story /
by Tim Champlin.—1st ed.
p. cm.
"A Five Star western"—T.p. verso.
ISBN 0-7862-3538-1 (hc : alk. paper)
1. Georgia—History—Civil War, 1861–1865—Fiction.
2. Western and Atlantic Railroad Company—Fiction.
3. Chattanooga Railroad Expedition, 1862—Fiction.
4. General (Locomotive)—Fiction. I. Title: Raiders of the
western and Atlantic. II. Title.
PS3553.H265 R35 2002

2002026603

For Dean Anderson, Audra Barber, and Twila Pettis,
heaven-sent care-givers who have enriched our lives

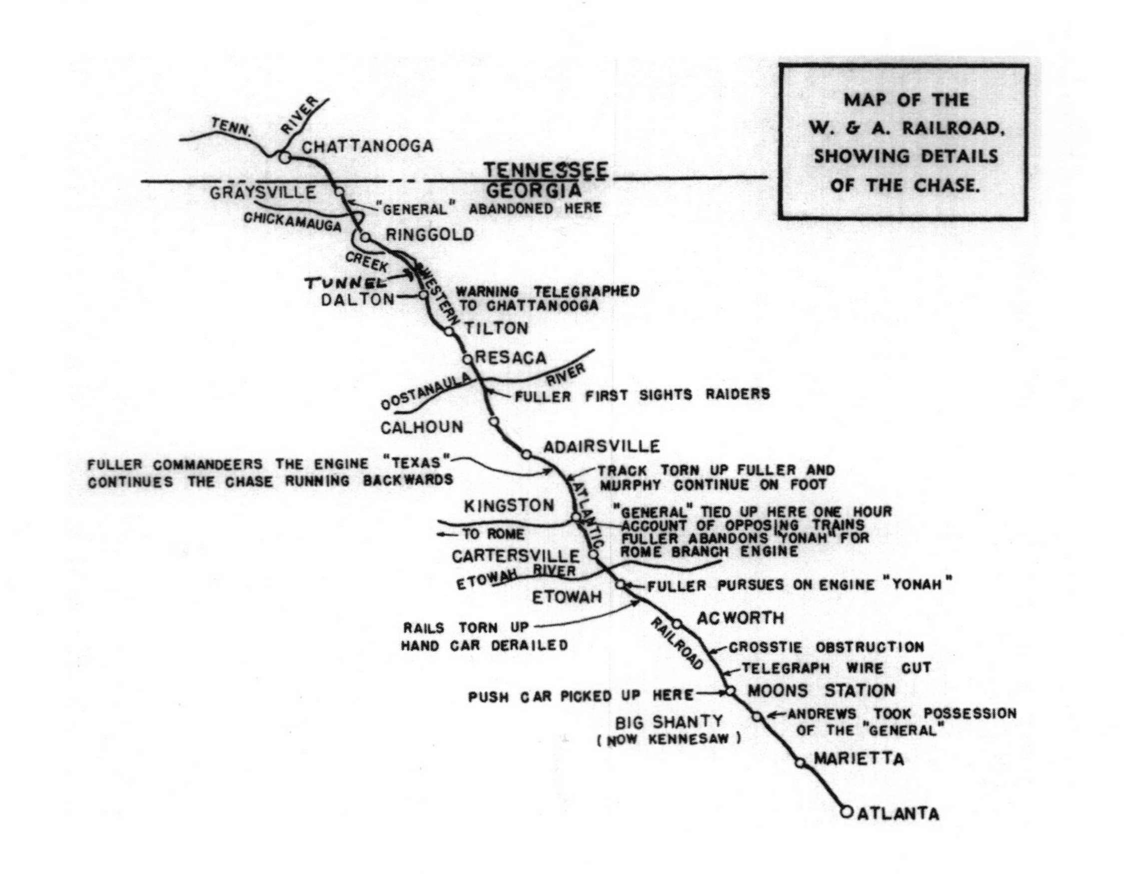
MAP OF THE
W. & A. RAILROAD,
SHOWING DETAILS
OF THE CHASE.
TENN.
RIVER
CHATTANOOGA
TENNESSEE
GEORGIA
GRAYSVILLE
"GENERAL" ABANDONED HERE
CHICKAMAUGA
RINGGOLD
CREEK
TUNNEL
DALTON
WESTERN
WARNING TELEGRAPHED
TO CHATTANOOGA
TILTON
RESACA
OOSTANAULA
RIVER
FULLER FIRST SIGHTS RAIDERS
CALHOUN
ADAIRSVILLE
FULLER COMMANDEERS THE ENGINE "TEXAS"
CONTINUES THE CHASE RUNNING BACKWARDS
TRACK TORN UP FULLER AND
MURPHY CONTINUE ON FOOT
ATLANTIC
KINGSTON
"GENERAL" TIED UP HERE ONE HOUR
ACCOUNT OF OPPOSING TRAINS
FULLER ABANDONS "YONAH" FOR
ROME BRANCH ENGINE
TO ROME
CARTERSVILLE
ETOWAH RIVER
ETOWAH
FULLER PURSUES ON ENGINE "YONAH"
RAILS TORN UP
HAND CAR DERAILED
ACWORTH
RAILROAD
CROSSTIE OBSTRUCTION
TELEGRAPH WIRE CUT
MOONS STATION
PUSH CAR PICKED UP HERE
BIG SHANTY
(NOW KENNESAW)
ANDREWS TOOK POSSESSION
OF THE "GENERAL"
MARIETTA
ATLANTA

Chapter One
a desperate plot
Ducktown, Georgia

Amelia Waymier had a flash of intuition, as if the sun had suddenly burst through the clouds to illuminate the dim dining room of her cavernous old house. Her heart began to pound and her hand shook as she replaced the coffee cup in the saucer.

"It's possible! I can do it!" she said, her voice sounding hollow in the empty room. Being alone these past months, she'd acquired the habit of thinking aloud. Not only did it clarify her thoughts, but it seemed to give her comfort — as if there were another presence in the room. "I'll steal that bullion right out from under the Rebs' noses and deliver it to the Yanks at Cartersville!" Her voice grew stronger with her resolve.

Pure folly! her inner voice scoffed.

But she merely smiled. Desperation had won this battle. Only a woman with little to lose would seriously consider such a scheme.

The source of her inspiration was two letters she'd collected that morning from the Ducktown post office. "You ain't had no mail for weeks, Miz Waymier," the balding clerk had said, reaching into the pigeonhole and handing over the wrinkled, water-stained envelopes. "Then you get two letters the very same day . . . from opposite directions."

She'd mumbled her thanks, tucked the letters into the side pocket of her cloak, and hurried out to her buggy, wondering how much this nosey clerk had seen of her mail.

Both letters now lay on the table beside her polished silver tea service. She'd read each several times, and would examine them again for any overlooked details. But the decision was made. Not for a moment did she consider her thought a wild flight of fancy or some kind of unattainable wish. She would do it, or be damned — shot or hanged. Failure was not a consideration. The venture would be the crowning achievement of her life — a life that had ceased to have much meaning or future, what with her rapidly dwindling resources and only fond memories of her late husband and absent sons to sustain her.

She took a deep breath to steady her nerves, stood up from the walnut dining room table, and paced to a tall window. Drawing aside the drapes, she was oblivious to the fine dust she shook loose from the heavy damask. The gray spring day just beyond the wavy, rain-streaked glass was a reflection of her life of late. But now all that was suddenly changed. Only in the last twenty minutes did she feel alive again, full of zeal and purpose. What remained was to turn this brilliant flash of an idea into a plan, a workable plan. And she had less than five days to work out the details and carry it through.

Not an impulsive woman by nature, she was a believer in certain signs and portents as well as in Divine Providence. Somehow, she meshed all unexplainable coincidences and gave them her own interpretation. Then she acted accordingly. The fact that the letters had arrived on the same day by different mail couriers, she took as a sign that their contents should be jointly acted upon.

One letter was from her favorite nephew, Lewis W. Quillian, who was now caretaker of the former United States mint at Dahlonega, Georgia, some twenty-five miles as the hawk flew to the northeast of where she sat. The steady, level-headed Quillian had worked at the mint, performing the jobs of coiner and assayer, since 1853. When the state of Georgia confiscated the mint and closed it down at the beginning of hostilities, Lewis Quillian was put in charge of overseeing the building and grounds until some other use could be found for the property. In his letter, he proudly stated that he'd just performed his most important duty as caretaker — casting seventeen gold bars, one hundred and ninety-six silver bars, and three others of mixed gold and silver. The raw metal had been deposited by the Confederate States government and was now being shipped by wagon, under armed escort, to the railroad at Marietta where the bullion would be sent south and east to Charleston.

Couched among Quillian's friendly concerns for her health and fortune was a request. He politely asked that the four soldiers who were driving the wagon and providing escort for the shipment be allowed to stop overnight at her house. He wasn't sure exactly when they would arrive, due to the state of the roads, but assumed it would be within three days following her receipt of his letter. Quillian thanked her in advance for her hospitality and stated that he would stand any expenses for food, lodging, or grain for the mules.

As she continued to stare out the window at the budding trees raising their bare limbs to the rain, she realized weather could play a part in her grand scheme. March and April were mud time in north Georgia. The unpaved back roads would be a quagmire of red goo, rutted with run-off or churned hub-deep by horse and wagon traffic. A freight wagon would be very difficult to manage in such conditions. More to the point, however, Quillian had named the four men who would be guarding the precious metal. Local boys all, two of them were not regular soldiers, but had been relegated to the home guard because of disabilities not sustained in the military. One, Rufus Riddell, had lost his sight on one side from a hunting accident when a faulty percussion cap exploded in his eye. In Amelia's opinion, the whole Riddell clan was not worth a bucket of pig slops. The other home guard was a chubby boy, John Carroll, who'd been born without a left hand and forearm. The other two she didn't know by name but were Confederate regulars who would accompany the shipment all the way to the depository in Charleston.

The second letter was from her youngest son, Josiah, a twenty-two-year-old private in the 2nd Ohio Volunteer Infantry, who had gone north eight months before to enlist. He had written the letter from camp near Murfreesboro, Tennessee. She could almost hear Josiah's excited voice speaking from the hastily scrawled lines on the paper. Seeing his handwriting gave her a pang of nostalgia as she remembered his dear past school days when she'd reviewed his written assignments. The words almost tumbled over each other as he proudly informed her of a special secret mission he'd volunteered for. Obviously he never considered this letter a breach of security because he wrote that many other soldiers knew about it, had volunteered, and been rejected. He was only one of twenty-one men chosen to go under cover into Georgia. They would steal a train near Atlanta and run it north along the Georgia State Road, burning bridges behind them to confound pursuit. Besides being eager for the adventure, he admitted that one of the main reasons he'd been chosen was his familiarity with the area along the Western & Atlantic rail line. He went on to state that he wasn't sure what the mission was designed to accomplish, but had heard rumors Chattanooga was to be attacked by Federal troops coming from the west. His daring raid and the burning of bridges would block any Rebel troops from moving north by rail to defend Chattanooga and east Tennessee. Josiah added that he knew this information would be safe with her because she had taught him to be a staunch Unionist.

"Little does he know," she muttered. With one grand gesture, she would avenge years of insults and false accusations she and her family had suffered at the hands of the Dahlonega citizens, she would strike a blow against the Confederacy, and she would escape from this place to finance her own future somewhere in the North.

With a feeling of satisfaction, she turned back from the window, and began to clear the few dishes from the long table. Even though she was alone, she still observed the formalities of setting the table, dressing properly, and taking every meal, including breakfast, in the spacious dining room. She caught herself listening for the chiming of the hall clock, which struck every quarter hour. Then, with a pang, she recalled she'd sold the tall clock last week to an antique dealer in order to settle her overdue tab at the grocer's.

Quite a contrast to the way she'd started out her adult life. Amelia Kitchings, debutante, had been introduced into Washington society thirty years ago. What a carefree time that had been. She'd eventually been courted, and won, by Albert Waymier. A Jew of German extraction, he'd been promptly disowned by his conservative family for marrying a Gentile in the Presbyterian Church. Cut off from his family's money, he'd spent most of his career working in various jobs in the Treasury Department while she stayed home and reared their two sons, Al, Jr. and Josiah.

Then, in 1853, under newly elected President Franklin Pierce, Albert had been offered the job as director of the United States branch mint at Dahlonega, Georgia. This had followed the removal of the local director named Davis after only two months on the job. She didn't know all the details of the furor that surrounded the previous director's removal, but, in hindsight, she wished they'd never moved South. It turned out to be a hornet's nest. Apparently the Dahlonega mint job had always been embroiled in politics, with the local people having a large say in who worked there.

The mid-1850s was a period when men were returning from the California gold fields. Most of them did not go back to mining the dwindling Georgia ore. Consequently coinage was down. But operational expenses at the mint went on. Worn equipment — such as scales and rolls — had to be replaced. The new rolls, from Pittsburgh, were not machined true and did not flatten the gold alloy strips to uniform thickness. Thus it was difficult to keep the weight of the coins within legal limits. Then there was the leaky roof that had to be fixed, the dilapidated outside fence replaced, boilers for the steam coining press repaired, and money paid out for ongoing salaries.

Albert, as good a manager and accountant as anyone could be, was resented by many local people. Amelia was convinced it was Albert's Northern dialect, his Jewish background, his strict adherence to Treasury Department regulations, and the fact that he was a Whig among States-Rights Democrats that caused local resentment. But most of all, the residents' anger smoldered because one of their own had not been appointed director. A campaign was begun to oust Albert. Unable to assail him on moral grounds, newspaper editorials and local businessmen accused him of mismanagement. Exaggeration and outright lies caused the Waymiers to become the least popular family in town. More than once, her two teenage sons came home from school with torn clothes and bloody noses from defending their family honor. Amelia had virtually no friends. People shunned them on the street.

After four tumultuous years, it was a relief to her when President Buchanan was elected in 1856, and Albert was replaced in early 1857. The two boys, now ages eighteen and twenty, moved out on their own just before Amelia and Albert left Dahlonega and bought a house thirty miles away in Ducktown. The two-story brick house had been constructed about the time the British burned Washington. Albert, retired and living on his savings, threw himself into repairing the old structure. They lived frugally and peacefully for two years until Albert began to suffer from heart trouble. Last summer, he'd dropped dead while weeding their garden, leaving her a widow at age fifty-one.

No life insurance and depleted savings had forced Amelia to begin selling off household items, furniture, and heirlooms to keep going. She was healthy and not above working, but had no history of working for wages and no skills. There were no factories in the vicinity. The poor whites couldn't afford to hire anything done, and the wealthier ones owned slaves to perform menial and domestic tasks. She was a decent seamstress, but more and more sewing was now done on the recently invented sewing machines.

As she heated water on the cook stove to wash the dishes, she longed to have her older son, Al, Jr., with her.

He, like her late husband, was a stocky, dark man with a practical side, good at fixing things. But, when the war started a year ago, he'd declared he wanted no part of this senseless killing, packed his saddlebags, and, with two companions, departed for Mexico. Amelia had not heard from him since, and wondered about his fate. Did he even know his father had died three months after he left?

But it was to Josiah, the slim, blond idealist and dreamer, that she turned her thoughts now. Even though he didn't yet know it, he and his fellow soldiers were to be part of her grand scheme — the recipients of the bullion shipment she would deliver to the stolen train.

Chapter Two

the raiders move out

Marietta, Georgia

"Time to rise, gentlemen! Your wake-up call!" The hotel porter's voice rumbled. Hard knuckles rattled the wooden door again, then footsteps receded down the hallway.

Gibson Carrick rolled over with a groan and slitted his eyelids toward the curtained window. Gray daylight filtered through soot-grimed glass, and he heard the chuffing of a locomotive somewhere below, followed by grinding brakes and the *hiss* of escaping steam.

He slipped out of bed while his six companions began to stir. Six men in two beds, and one more on the floor — it was enough to keep a man from getting any comfortable sleep. But he was a soldier, as they all were. Having recently bivouacked in leaky tents, barns, and roadside ditches open to the pelting rain, by comparison this was almost luxury.

Carrick poured water from pitcher to bowl on a bedside stand and dashed cupped handfuls into his face, rubbing his gritty eyes. Lacking a towel, he dried his face with the sleeve of his long underwear. During four hours of restless sleep, he'd at least been spared thoughts or dreams of the perilous mission they were about to undertake. Now the awareness rushed in and his stomach tensed with anticipation once again. To one degree or another, their nerves were strained from several days of trekking afoot by twos and threes through southern Tennessee and northern Georgia disguised as civilians on their way to enlist in the Southern forces. Continuous rain and mud had slowed their journey. Finally, in order to keep their rendezvous at Marietta on Friday, April 11, 1862, eight of them had been forced to catch a southbound train at Ringgold, Georgia, twelve miles from Chattanooga. Reaching this trackside hotel in Marietta well after midnight, they checked in and got what sleep they could before the clerk pounded them awake. Twenty-two in number, they were scattered among three rooms in this hotel and one room at a hotel across the tracks.

"Short night," Private Mark Wood muttered, sitting on the edge of the bed in his long johns and scrubbing a hand over his face. The bristles of his drooping mustache stuck out at odd angles to match his black, curly hair.

The other men were mostly silent, pulling on their pants, sliding galluses over their shoulders, yawning, and rubbing the sleep from their eyes. William Pittenger, clean-shaven corporal of the 2nd Ohio Volunteer Infantry, appeared solemn and alert, as if he'd not slept at all. He secured the bows of his wire-rimmed glasses behind each ear. The spectacles and his longish brown hair gave Bill Pittenger the appearance of a stern schoolmaster about to face a classroom of unruly students. Carrick studied the young man's face for a moment and recalled how eagerly Pittenger had volunteered for this mission, as if afraid he wouldn't see enough action in Tennessee, or maybe he was just hoping to do his part to end the war quickly. Could be that Pittenger's serious mien was only masking the fear of what this day would bring. He might be having second thoughts about volunteering, now that the moment was nearly at hand. If so, he wasn't alone.

Carrick slid his arms into the sleeves of his pale blue shirt. Only a week ago all of them had been wearing blue — Federal blue. Now it was just butternut and overalls, muddy boots and slouch hats, so they would blend into the population. There was no distinguishing a sergeant-major from a private. Young men all, Carrick saw them as mature, battle-hardened veterans who had somehow come unscathed through numerous bloody skirmishes. He, himself, had left a good job as a railroad dispatcher in Paducah, Kentucky to enlist in an Ohio regiment just after hostilities began. Now, a year later, he'd volunteered for this mission as his chance to help shorten the war.

Elihu Mason looked older because of his full beard and his lack of a sense of humor. He spent much time alone, reading his pocket Testament. The three other men in the room, Sergeant William Campbell, Sergeant-Major Marion Ross, and Private Samuel Robertson, each wore stylish chin whiskers with a clean upper lip, much like their Commander-in-Chief, President Abraham Lincoln. Private Sam Robertson, in spite of the narrow, carefully cultivated beard rimming his chin, appeared the most youthful of the group, and was probably the most reckless as well.

Carrick sat down on the only chair in the room to pull on his high, black boots. The clammy, mud-stiffened leather smelled of mildew. As he stamped his feet into them, he wondered if he would be able to run in this footgear, if the necessity arose. Doubtful. He felt a sudden aversion to all this. Why was he even here? He would have given almost anything to be some place else right now — any place, that is, except where he'd come from. As a corporal, he'd so far known little but the usual military fare — marching in all kinds of weather, subject to camp fever and dysentery, eating hardtack and half-raw bacon, trying to keep his paper cartridges and socks dry. There was nothing quite like the bottomless feeling in his stomach when the band struck up some patriotic air, leading the ranks toward a Confederate breastworks where the boys in gray awaited them with thunderous death.

A slight shudder went over him at the recollection. Well, at least he'd put off marrying, so had no worry about a wife and children at home. He took a deep breath and stood up. All of them had eagerly volunteered for an under cover assignment that would relieve them of their usual onerous and deadly duty. Dozens of men had been turned away. What criteria the officers and the civilian leader, James J. Andrews, had used to select them, Carrick didn't know. Yet, he was grateful he'd been included in this disparate group. It wasn't necessary that they get along; it was only required that they work together under discipline for a short time.

"Wish I had some coffee," Private Robertson growled, looking owlish.

"One night in a hotel, and he's asking for room service!" Sergeant-Major Ross chuckled.

The comment broke the palpable tension in the room, and several men laughed.

"If you're placing an order, I'll take some ham and eggs," Mark Wood said.

"White flour biscuits and gravy for me," chimed in Sergeant Campbell, licking his lips.

Robertson, the butt of the joke, grew red in the face, but apparently his military discipline kept him from lashing out at Sergeant-Major Ross, even though Ross was from another company and not normally his superior. The young private had a hair-trigger. Rail-thin, Robertson could have used several good meals. He'd probably enlisted from some poor dirt farm in Ohio in hopes the Army would provide him with enough to eat.

"I wasn't askin' for no gawd-damn' room service," Robertson grumbled. "Camp coffee would do for me." He slapped the dust out of his corduroy coat and put it on, not looking at the beefy Sergeant-Major Ross.

"Seriously, are we going to get breakfast before we start?" Pittenger asked.

"There's an eatin' place downstairs if we don't waste too much time here," the jovial, round-faced Sergeant Campbell said, sliding a small timepiece out of his watch pocket.

At that moment came a discreet rap at the door. Carrick opened it a crack, then swung it inward, and twelve more men shuffled quietly into the room, led by James J. Andrews, the man all of them recognized as their leader. Carrick closed the door behind them, and turned the key in the lock.

"Gather 'round. There's no hurry yet. It still lacks a little of train time," Andrews said.

They flowed around into a rough circle, filling the room, and making it seem much smaller. Four of them sat on the edges of the beds; others leaned against the window sash.

Andrews tossed his hat onto a rumpled bed, pulled the wooden chair to him, and propped a booted foot on it. For some reason none of them knew, Andrews was not a military man. He functioned as a civilian spy. A strong Union sympathizer, he had been a house painter and schoolteacher in the small town of Flemingsburg, Kentucky, although it was rumored he was a native of Hancock County in western Virginia. He was certainly a striking figure in appearance — about thirty years old and six feet tall with a heavy build. He wore a neatly trimmed and brushed brown beard, with a clean-shaven upper lip. A long, straight nose and clear eyes, combined to give him an intelligent, honest appearance. He had an air of serene confidence and qualities of leadership that gained him the absolute trust of military officers and enlisted men alike. Just now he was dressed in a gray frock coat, vest, white cotton shirt and cravat, pin-stripe pants, and polished boots.

"Boys, you were briefed when I recruited you, so there's not much to say," he began, looking at the alert group. "We're entering on a very hazardous expedition, but it will have a glorious ending. We'll give the enemy the deadliest blow he's yet received. Focus on the job ahead. Just think how good it will feel to run through the South, leaving the bridges burning and Rebs in helpless rage behind us! If we destroy those bridges as we go north, General Mitchell will capture Chattanooga the very next day, and all east Tennessee will be open in front of him. We have to be prompt. If Mitchell's troops get to Huntsville before we do, the rails will be so crowded with reinforcements moving against him, our job will be a lot harder. But if we have the bridges down first, the Rebs can't send a force against him, and Mitchell's men will have everything their own way. Our timing is critical. Everyone understand what's at stake?"

There was a general nodding and murmuring of assent.

"Get seats near each other in the same car and don't discuss the matter among yourselves. When the train stops at Big Shanty for breakfast, keep your places till I tell you to go. If anything unexpected happens, look to me for the word. Bill Knight" — he pointed at a blue-eyed man next to him — "will go with me on the locomotive. He's an experienced engineer. When I give the order, all the rest of you will come up on the left of the train, forward of where it's uncoupled, and climb on the cars wherever you can find room. If anybody interferes, shoot him, but don't fire until it's necessary."

Sergeant-Major Marion Ross, the ranking man of the party, raised a hand. "I respectfully suggest we postpone the attempt . . . or give it up altogether."

Surprised and curious glances were turned in his direction. Andrews silently waited for him to continue.

"Several reasons," he went on. "Circumstances have changed since we set out. More troops and new recruits are camped at Big Shanty, and we noticed the crowded state of the road as we came down. General Mitchell's movement eastward toward Chattanooga is going to draw a quick response, and that one-track railroad north is going to be jammed with soldiers."

"Everything you say is correct," Andrews replied. "But with all the military excitement and the number of trains on the road it's less likely our train will be suspected once we get going. If we work quickly, the troops at Big Shanty won't have time to interfere. We'll snatch the train and be off before they realize what's happened. The element of surprise is all on our side. There will be no guard on the train because who would suspect it could be stolen while parked next to a military camp?"

"Why Big Shanty instead of right here in Marietta?"

"Because Big Shanty is a breakfast stop for the train crew. And there's no telegraph there for anyone to send the alarm on ahead of us."

Andrews seemed to have an answer for everything, but Carrick could think of several flaws in the plan. Three others voiced their misgivings. The first flush f enthusiasm among the recruits was giving way to doubts, now that the critical time was at hand. A man named J. A. Wilson respectfully, but forcefully, objected to proceeding with the plan. "It's just too dangerous," he concluded.

"Audacious, you mean," countered Andrews. "I'm dressed in these fine clothes because I'm posing as an official of the Western and Atlantic Railroad. I have a fake letter in my pocket that gives me authority to run this train, supposedly pulling three boxcars of ammunition, through to General Beauregard. Instead, you men will be hiding in those cars. If anyone challenges us, let me do the talking. If anything should go wrong, and you are caught or questioned, just remember to say that you're from Flemingsburg, Kentucky and you came south to enlist in a Confederate regiment. I'm from Flemingsburg. It's a small place and I know everyone there, so they can't trip you up on your story." He paused and looked at the individual faces around him. "We planned this once before three weeks ago with another group, but had to abort the operation before it got started. This time, I'll either succeed or leave my bones in Dixie!" His voice was low, but intense. "Anyone who isn't with me, can stay in this hotel and make his way back north as best he can."

Carrick could see that most were thrilled and inspired by the words. Those with objections simply shrugged and dropped their heads in resignation.

"All right, then, it's almost train time. Let's go!"

Chapter Three
confidence game
Ducktown, Georgia

"Help yourselves, gentlemen," Amelia Waymier urged. "There's plenty."

"Believe I'll have another drumstick and more biscuits and gravy," Rufus Riddell said, stretching a skinny arm across the table for the platter of golden brown chicken.

Amelia sat at the head of the dining room table and beamed on the four men. Her congenial motherly charm concealed her private thoughts. Rufus Riddell was just as thin and dirty as ever. His lank black hair looked as if it'd been haggled off just below his ears and he was dressed in a cast-off gray uniform coat that was too large for his bony frame. Other than that, he looked nearly the same as when she'd last seen him more than a year before in Dahlonega. She tried not to stare at the one milky blind eye he turned in her direction as she passed the gravy boat. Even though it was an insult to the animal, she always thought Rufus bore a strong resemblance to a weasel.

From the way they were all putting away the food, she deduced they'd not eaten a home-cooked meal in weeks. John Carroll, the other member of the home guard, his lower left sleeve pinned up where his forearm and hand were missing, had lost most of his boyish chubbiness, but he still had a round baby face, devoid of whiskers and chapped to a rosy hue by exposure.

The other two men, Confederate regulars, wore trail-stained gray uniforms. Although young, they seemed much more mature alongside the two home guards. These regulars had introduced themselves as Sergeant Bill Farrell and Corporal Jack Hyde. The corporal had red hair and was attempting to grow a mustache. The sergeant had dark, curly hair. Neither man had shaved in several days, giving them a scruffy appearance. At least she'd seen to it that they washed their faces and hands before coming to the table. She'd given them a towel and lye soap to take out to the cold water pump in the dooryard.

"Miz Waymier, this is the best food I've had since I left home," Corporal Hyde said, nodding his head as she passed him a bottle of red wine.

"Nothing I like better than to see a man with a good appetite . . . unless it's four men with good appetites." She smiled, watching with satisfaction as he refilled his wine glass.

For the occasion, she'd killed her only remaining laying hen and the rooster, peeled fifteen sprouting potatoes, and prepared a sumptuous dinner consisting of fried chicken, two jars of last summer's stewed tomatoes from the root cellar, mashed potatoes and gravy and biscuits. She'd washed and ironed the linen tablecloth, thankful she hadn't yet been forced to sell her only set of good china.

The men were obviously awed by her taste and manners and the spread she'd set before them. Rufus Riddell was still the low-life he'd always been, but John Carroll seemed self-conscious about his dirty clothes and muddy boots. The Carrolls had some breeding. Amelia almost felt sorry for this crippled boy.

She kept up a friendly chatter as the meal progressed, commenting on the weather and the state of the roads. Not once did she mention the load they were carrying.

As they'd pulled the loaded wagon into her barn just before dark and unhitched the mules, she tried to get a peek at the load under the canvas cover without being obvious. But the oiled canvas was lashed down on all sides. The men had rubbed down the wet mules with dry rags, then forked down some hay into the stalls to go with the bait of grain she had for them. When all was secure, Sergeant Farrell asked if there was a lock for the barn door.

"Lord, no! Just that crossbar that slides into place to keep the doors shut."

He'd frowned, but muttered something to the effect that he reckoned it would be safe enough overnight.

Amelia's plan seemed to be progressing nicely for the moment as she presided at table. She had them all eating and drinking — especially drinking — and off their guard, thinking they were secure.

Her late husband had attempted to lay in a stock of various vintages to build up a wine cellar before good wines became more expensive and difficult to obtain. When he died, there were only a half dozen dusty bottles left on the wooden rack in the cellar. Amelia knew white wine from red, but that was about the extent of it. It didn't matter that she was no connoisseur, neither were her guests. For this dinner she opened four bottles at random to be sure they hadn't turned to vinegar. Three of them were different kinds of dry red wine and the fourth was a heavy, sweet sherry. She had no idea how much these aged bottles were worth to a collector, but they'd been next on her list of items to sell for operating cash. The fact that she still had them and the contents were drinkable were signs that this alcohol was meant to serve a greater purpose.

"Miz Waymier, ma'am, when Lewis told us you'd be putting us up for the night, I never expected nothin' like this," Carroll said, around a mouthful of potatoes and gravy.

"That's fer sure," Riddell added, dropping a chicken bone on his plate. Ignoring the linen napkin, he wiped his greasy hands on his pants.

Amelia smiled her pleasure, and smoothed down the frilly white apron that was sewn as a decorative front to her long, pale blue dress. Her short, graying hair was stylishly coifed and held in place by tortoise shell combs. She'd been careful not to overdress. Even if she hadn't already sold her jewelry, she would not have flaunted it in front of these men. Simple hospitality with a touch of elegance — that was the impression she sought to create.

"When Lewis Quillian said his aunt would be putting us up, I figured maybe we'd get a sandwich and a cup of coffee and be sleepin' in the barn," Corporal Hyde commented, setting down his long-stemmed wine glass on the white tablecloth with the care of someone slightly tipsy. "Never imagined we'd be treated like royalty. Makes riding in rain and mud almost worth it to get vittles like this." He paused to rip off a mouthful of chicken. "Yes, sir," he said, chewing, "I reckon some o' them jaspers thought we was getting the short end of the stick when we was assigned to escort that wagonload of. . . ."

"Of Gatling gun ammunition," Sergeant Farrell finished with a sharp look at the corporal. "A hundred thousand rounds of belted cartridges."

Amelia put down her fork and dabbed at her mouth with a napkin. "Sergeant, you needn't try to hide the fact that your load consists of gold and silver bars from the mint."

She smiled at his look of consternation. "My nephew told me he cast those ingots. I haven't mentioned it to anyone, but I'm sure it's not a big secret. Things like that have a way of leaking out. It stands to reason some Dahlonega people saw wagons coming and going, saw smoke from the smelter, then the armed guard, and figured out you have a valuable cargo." She shrugged dismissively and broke a biscuit. "I hardly think you're in any danger. Folks in Georgia are all loyal to the cause. I'm sure everyone wants to see that money spent on food or goods from France or England."

"Well, there are a lot of robbers on the roads, even in the South, who are not loyal to the cause. They're going to take advantage of the war to enrich themselves any way they can," Sergeant Farrell said, his face darkening under the stubble of beard.

"Well, as a practical matter, it doesn't seem likely anyone would attempt to steal such a cargo, if those gold and silver bars are as heavy as I imagine them to be," Amelia said lightly. "I'm sure you are quite safe from any gangs of deserters or road agents who might be roaming the hills of north Georgia. Besides, you have only another twenty or thirty miles to put it on the train, depending on which way you're headed."

"Huh!" the sergeant snorted. "You wouldn't believe how long it's taken us just to get this far." He smothered a pile of mashed potatoes with a ladle of giblet gravy. "Mud up to our eyeballs, bogging down the mules and wagon, bridges washed out, causing detours or long delays before we could ford the creeks. We could've crossed the whole state in the time it's taken us to go thirty miles."

Amelia murmured her sympathetic understanding. As the meal continued, she kept the conversation on the light side, carefully observing how much wine the men drank. Thank goodness none of them was a teetotaler. By the time she brought the fourth bottle from the sideboard, she could see the men were much more relaxed, wiping up the last of the food and slouching in their chairs. Even Sergeant Farrell, who had been wary at first, seemed to be unbending. He was no longer regarding her with suspicious looks as he had since he'd caught her trying to peer under the canvas wagon cover.

She disappeared into the kitchen for her culinary *coup de grâce*.

"That sherry will go well with dessert," she declared, reappearing with large wedges of fresh-baked apple pie.

"Oh, my! I didn't leave room for that!" Corporal Hyde exclaimed. "But I'll sure give it a try!" he vowed, easing his belt loose.

She took her place and pretended to eat, although she'd consumed only enough to satisfy her hunger, barely sipping at a small glass of wine during the course of the evening.

A half hour later, the four men and their hostess retired to the back parlor with their refilled glasses of sherry. Earlier in the day Amelia had laid a fire on the hearth and now lighted it to knock off the damp chill in the room, and to provide some light. She also lighted the coal-oil lamp on a side table. Lounging with their drinks on the stuffed chairs and sofa, two of the men lighted pipes, settling in comfortably. The burning hickory and oak spread an aromatic warmth through the parlor.

They had long since exhausted any topics of common interest. The desultory conversation flagged, and finally ceased. Rufus Riddell and John Carroll leaned their heads back on the sofa and dozed off, their regular breathing the only sound in the room except for the shifting of logs in the fireplace.

Finally, with an effort, Sergeant Farrell heaved himself erect. "Ma'am, I want to thank you for your hospitality, but we've got to set a night guard on the wagon. Then the rest of us need to get some sleep. I want to be on the road early."

"But I've prepared bedrooms for you to sleep upstairs, Sergeant," she said in a disappointed tone.

"Got to post a guard," he mumbled, adjusting his wrinkled tunic and tugging his holstered gun into place. "Two of us will sleep in the barn and alternate watches."

Her stomach tensed. This might prove difficult. "No need of that," she said smoothly, secretly fearful that all her careful planning was about to go awry because of one cautious, dutiful sergeant. She didn't want to play her ace — a double-barreled shotgun — unless she got desperate. "Nobody knows you're here," she continued in a soothing voice. "That wagon will be perfectly safe in the barn."

He hesitated, hand resting on the flap of his holster, fatigue heavy in his face.

She quickly followed up her advantage. "When's the next time you'll have a chance to sleep in a warm bed with clean sheets?" she asked. "All of you will be a lot more rested for the remainder of your trip."

She could see him wearily trying to concentrate, to weigh the options and the risk. Nature came to her rescue in the form of a flicker of lightning that briefly lighted the back window. It was followed a few seconds later by a grumble of distant thunder.

"I'll keep an eye on the barn," Amelia said, turning away as if that settled the matter. "It's fixin' to storm and I don't sleep well when it's storming. You can bet nobody will be out in this kind of weather. This house is two miles from town."

"I'm obliged," he finally consented, pulling out his pocket watch. "It's only half past nine, but I'm getting these boys to bed. Then we can be up and out of here before daylight." He shoved the watch out of sight. "Come on, Corporal, roust up these two sleeping beauties. Time to hit the hay. Rufus! John! Shake it out of there!"

"I'll show you to your rooms," Amelia said, breathing her relief as she took the lamp from the table. She paused in the entrance hall at the foot of the staircase. "I'd appreciate it if you'd leave your muddy boots down here. I'll see if I can clean them up some. Maybe put some boot black and oil on them."

"Thanks, but not necessary, ma'am," Farrell said.

"I want to. Besides," — she smiled — "then I'll be sure there's no dirt on my bedclothes or carpets up there."

"Very well, then," he agreed. They tugged off each other's boots and set them aside.

She led the way up the creaking stairs with the lamp held high, shadows wavering along the walls and into the dark corners. The men shuffled silently behind her on stockinged feet.

"These two rooms right here, side-by-side." She opened the door to one of them, went in, and lighted the lamp on a side table.

"Corporal, you and I will take this one," Sergeant Farrell said. "John and Rufus can have the other one."

The three men he addressed were too befuddled by wine and food and their short nap to reply.

"Good night, then," Amelia said. "I'll have some breakfast and coffee ready early in the morning to see you on your way." As she retreated down the stairs, lightning flashed again, illuminating a pale oval in the beveled glass of the front door.

She collected the four pairs of dirty boots and carried them into the lean-to that served as a back porch. She'd think of some good place to hide them later. Then she returned to the back parlor, shoved another log onto the dying fire, and sat down to wait. She consulted the tiny gold Elgin she wore pinned to her waistband — it was only 9:45 — and closed the case. Every time she looked at the watch, she thought of Albert who had given this to her on their twenty-fifth wedding anniversary. For a moment, a terrible sense of loneliness overcame her. The years were deceptive. They passed slowly, nearly imperceptibly, until she awoke one day to find that most of her life was past, her family and friends either dead or scattered, her finances rapidly declining.

But she was convinced that there was a purpose to everything that happened. All things in her life that had gone before were only small steps leading inevitably to this place and this time and this set of circumstances. She settled into the armchair, comfortable with the thought of what she was about to do. It was predestined, as her Presbyterian beliefs had taught her. What others called superstition, she saw as her ability to recognize and act on signs and portents to carry out the will of God. The fact that she was about to steal a wagonload of gold and silver worth hundreds of thousands of dollars, she saw as a justifiable act of war. After all, it had been smelted and cast at the former United States mint and she was merely returning the bullion to its rightful owners, the Federal government — and taking a fee for her services.

She turned her thoughts to the practicalities of what she had to do. Originally she'd considered disarming the men and locking them in the root cellar. She'd found no plausible excuse to lure them all into the root cellar at once — and no opportunity to disarm them. She *had* prevailed on them to leave their Spencer carbines in the lean-to, but they'd insisted on wearing their sidearms to the table.

She'd thought of trying to bribe them with several gold bars to look the other way while she made off with the remainder, and they reported it stolen. But she quickly dismissed this idea as too chancy. She had to know in advance that all four would be amenable to a bribe before she tipped her hand. Anyone who would take a bribe could not be trusted to be satisfied with only that. They could easily hide the bribe, and arrest her for stealing. Or, if inclined to thievery, they could make off with the entire shipment themselves, hide it in the wooded hills, and disappear.

No, guile was the best way. She had their boots, and she would take her own mule, along with their team and wagon, leaving them afoot to walk the two miles to the village. They still had their pistols, but she had all four of the Spencer repeaters they'd left in the lean-to. Could they catch her on horseback? No doubt about it. The most she could hope for was about a twelve-hour head start. They would be angry and humiliated that an elderly woman had flim-flammed them. Since she was a female, they might not shoot her on sight if they overtook the wagon; they'd probably save her for the hangman. But she knew she was not destined to fail.

Lightning flashed again, and the thunder crashed, louder and closer now, a spring storm rolling in from the west. It would be a close thing. She had to wait long enough for them to be dead asleep, then slip out to the barn where she'd stashed some male attire to travel in. She would even take some cold fried chicken and a couple of biscuits to keep up her strength. To have any chance of success, she would have to reach the road without waking Sergeant Farrell — the only one who seemed the least bit alert.

She was used to handling mules, and the team had been rubbed down, fed both hay and grain and rested now for four hours. Not enough to be fully restored, but maybe they would prove more docile if they were still a little tired. The men had even pumped buckets of water and washed down the mules' legs and bellies to prevent mud fever.

The storm would be both good and bad. Thunder would help mask any noises she or the animals made in the barn, or the rattling of trace chains. But lightning at the wrong moment could reveal her to eyes watching from a second-story window. The rain would wash out any tracks, but would also turn the road to clinging mud. She had to go four miles before the fork in the road, one turning south-west toward Marietta and Atlanta, the other continuing west to Cartersville. Cartersville, about twenty miles from here along the Western & Atlantic, was a wooding and water stop for northbound trains. If she could average even two miles an hour, she could make it in ten hours — just about the amount of a head start she expected to have.

But what if she reached Cartersville undetected? What then? Her son, Josiah, had written that he and the other conspirators were to steal the train on Saturday, April 12th. This was already Friday, the 11th. She had to be at the Cartersville wood yard fairly early tomorrow morning. That would give her just about ten hours to make the twenty miles. It should be sufficient, barring some calamity.

Might as well get busy to kill some time, she thought, getting up and going out into the lean-to. What to do with the boots? She had a sudden idea. Uncovering a big crock tub of hog lard, she took a small wooden paddle and began scooping the soft lard into the boots, packing it down into the toes. When she'd finished, she went outside, heaved up the slanted plank door to the root cellar, and tossed the heavy footgear down into the blackness. "That should slow them up some," she muttered to herself, easing the door back into place.

Then she took the four Spencer carbines from the lean-to, wrapped them in one of Albert's old overcoats, and carried them to the barn. Quietly sliding the bar back, she opened one of the big doors just far enough to slip inside with the rifles. She wished she had made some sort of fastener for the inside of the doors, but too late to think of that now.

Even in the blackness she knew by long familiarity the location of everything. She felt for a coal-oil lantern hanging from its accustomed peg, took it down, and lighted it. Even with the wick turned low, the light would show through the cracks in the old barn. She shielded the lantern inside an empty stall, then went into the tack room and removed a bundle of rolled-up clothing from a burlap feed sack. Working quickly, she changed from her dress, shift, and high, lace-up shoes into the denim pants and wool flannel shirt, then tugged on a pair of well-oiled boots. Lastly she yanked out the tortoise shell combs, swept back her hair, and tied it with a blue ribbon. A broad-brimmed black felt hat topped the outfit. She stuffed her dress and shoes into the sack.

She untied the wagon cover, and threw it back. Holding the lantern close to the stacked wooden crates, she read the black stenciling on the sides — **.45 Cal. Gatling Belted Cartridges. Property CSA**.

Just as Sergeant Farrell had said. She was startled. Was she mistaken about this cargo? Had her nephew misled her?

Maybe there was another shipment coming. But, no, Lewis Quillian had named the four men who were escorting the bullion, and it was the same four who were now occupying her upstairs bedrooms. It must be a ruse to throw off any curious eyes.

A brilliant flash of lightning illuminated every crack in the front of the old building. It was quickly doused by a mighty crash of thunder. She had to hurry. She'd already devised a plan of her own to disguise the load further from any prying eyes, and that was to pile cordwood on top of the crates to make it appear as if the whole wagon were filled with firewood. But now she hesitated. The boxes were disguised already, and the cordwood would make the heavy wagon heavier. Would the axles tolerate it? Could the mules pull it through the mud she was sure to encounter? If anyone stopped her, she could still say she was delivering a load of ammunition to the railroad for shipment. But a woman alone without any soldiers? She had no papers. In the unlikely event that anyone challenged her, she'd have to bluff her way through.

Forget the wood. That change of plan would save much time and energy. She unrolled the overcoat and unloaded three of the Spencers by drawing the tube full of cartridges out through the metal butt plates. Then she rewrapped the three empty weapons in the overcoat and his them under a pile of straw in an empty stall. Keeping one loaded carbine and the three extra tubes of cartridges, she slid it into the burlap sack with her good clothes, and shoved the sack under the wagon seat.

Harnessing the strange mules was no problem for her; she had been used to hitching and unhitching both mules and horses most of her life. Slowly, carefully she backed the mules out of their stalls and into place. As she was hooking up the doubletree, a crash of thunder ushered in a rush of wind and rain as the storm burst around the barn. A low roar of rain pounded on the wooden shingles far above, and dribbles of water began dripping through in several dozen places, accentuating the odor of musty hay and ammonia. She tied her own mule on a long tether to the back of the wagon.

Suddenly she heard a banging noise, as if something had fallen. She froze and listened for several long seconds. Nothing. She let out her breath and resumed her work. Again she heard it above the noise. Something outside.

She quickly snuffed the lantern and crept toward the barn door, eased it open a crack, and peered out — only blackness and the chilling rain slanting sideways in the wind. A flash of lightning wavered just long enough for her to look at the upstairs bedroom windows. As were many of the early structures, the old house was only one room thick, so she had had no choice about putting the soldiers into bedrooms at the front of the house. But she had taken the early precaution of closing the outside shutters. Another lightning flash revealed what she had feared. The shutter from Sergeant Farrell's room stood ajar. Just as the lightning flamed out, she saw the wind flap the white shutter against the brick house. It was this noise she'd heard. Would the thunder wake the men? Would the banging shutter arouse them? She eased the barn door shut, her heart suddenly racing. She fumbled for the lantern, carried it into an open stall, and re-lighted it, turning it low, barely illuminating the hitching. Now her hands were shaking with anxiety and haste.

Finally she straightened up with a deep breath as she completed the job. The mules stood, docile in harness. Was everything ready? What had she forgotten? She slipped out her watch, took the tiny key suspended from its chain, and wound it. Ten after eleven. She put the watch away, and her breathing steadied. What else? Food! That was it. She'd set out some fried chicken, biscuits, and a big canteen of water in the kitchen. But did she dare go back for it? Yes. She swung her traveling cape around her and tossed the oversize hood up over her felt hat. Then she retrieved Albert's double-barreled shotgun from the tack room, freshly loaded and capped this morning. She snuffed the lantern, and put it under the seat of the wagon. Then, holding the shotgun under her long cape out of the wet, she pushed open the barn door. The spring storm still raged outside; frequent lightning showed the wind whipping the rain in sideways sheets. Nothing in sight. She prayed that all four men were dead asleep. It was said that the heaviest part of sleep came in the first three hours after eating and imbibing heavily. She had to count on it being so.

To prevent temporary blindness, she closed her eyes until the next lightning flash blinked out, then hurried across the yard. She retrieved the food, wrapped in a linen napkin, and stuffed it into her side pocket. Pausing in the darkness of the lean-to and allowing her breathing and heartbeat to slow, she experienced a slight twinge of regret at leaving this old house and all of her remaining possessions, especially her silver tea service and her books. But one couldn't gain new things without letting go of the old.

Shaking the rain off her cape, she got a better grip on the shotgun, pushed open the door, and started back to the barn. Halfway across the dooryard, a brilliant lightning flash lit up the house, the outbuildings, and everything in between. She sucked in her breath, feeling like a mouse caught out of its hole. But she made the barn and slipped inside, praying she had not been seen.

The patient mules stood in harness in the musty-smelling darkness. Thunder boomed hollowly, less threateningly, outside as the storm slowly moved off to the east.

Go now! a silent voice urged her. The team was facing the big double doors as she swung one open, then the other. She climbed to the wagon seat, laying the shotgun at her feet, and unwrapped the reins from the long brake handle. Never having driven a six-mule hitch, she was having trouble in the blackness sorting out the lines to thread between her fingers.

A long, wavering lightning flash lit up the huge square where the doors were propped open, causing the mules to shift nervously.

"What the hell are you doing?" Sergeant Farrell's voice boomed.

The shock nearly stopped her heart as her eyes flicked up and she caught the silhouette of a hatted figure in the doorway.

But the paralysis lasted only a half second. The reins were bunched in her hands and she popped them over the mules' backs. "Hyah! Giddap! Go!"

The sudden noise and the stinging leather lines caused the nervous mules to leap ahead, almost throwing her over the back of the low seat as they lunged into the traces. The big wagon thundered ahead out the door and into the darkness. Rattling, banging, snorting, they flew across the yard, Amelia praying they wouldn't run into the pump before she could get control of the team. A shout sounded faintly from behind, then a pistol cracked. She hunched forward, yelling, and lashed the panicked mules with the wet reins. Another shot banged, and the lead slug tugged at her hat brim, as the iron-rimmed wagon wheels slewed dangerously in the mud.

A flash of lightning showed they were already past the corner of the house, onto the carriage drive. She desperately fumbled to sort out the reins and pull the near side mules toward the west road. She finally got the right three reins and yanked hard. The wagon slid sideways and bumped over the uneven ground, as the powerful mules came around to the right, then shot ahead down the road, leaving Sergeant Farrell and his bootless companions afoot in the darkness of the storm.

Chapter Four

snatching the general

Marietta, Georgia

J. J. Andrews's men dispersed from the second-story room in the Fletcher House. There was no time to find the hotel dining room. The train was due to depart in fifteen minutes and would stop for breakfast at Big Shanty, eight miles up the line. To further the ruse that all these men were strangers, traveling separately, Andrews had earlier bought and handed out several tickets to places like Adairsville, Dalton, and Ringgold. Gibson Carrick, along with the remaining six who still needed tickets, queued up at the barred ticket window of the depot next door.

As Josiah Waymier turned away from the station agent's cage, Carrick was able to catch his eye. A look of recognition passed between them. For several days, Carrick and Waymier had traveled on foot together making their way south from Shelbyville, Tennessee, sleeping in barns and hedgerows, and walking the railroad tracks to avoid the boggy roads. Carrick had taken an instinctive liking to the slim, blond youngster. Unfailingly cheerful and optimistic, Waymier was a valuable traveling companion in other respects. Having spent several of his growing-up years in Georgia, he knew the people and their ways. When he and Carrick sought overnight shelter at some farmhouse,

Waymier always put their hosts at ease with his friendly manner and convincing story that they were on their way south from Flemingsburg, Kentucky to join the Confederate Army.

Carrick paid for his ticket to Cartersville with a half eagle, pocketed his change, then made his way casually outside into the damp April morning. The targeted locomotive stood panting softly at the platform, beads of condensation glistening in the first shafts of sunlight. The black American-type 4-4-0 engine featured a balloon stack, shining brass trim, and two five-foot tall driving wheels on each side, trimmed in red to match the cab and the cowcatcher. On the side of the boiler was mounted a brass plate with the word *General* several inches high in bold relief.

The train consisted of locomotive and tender, followed by three empty boxcars with the doors open, then two passenger coaches, and a caboose.

Yawning a feigned indifference to fellow travelers, Carrick stepped up into the first passenger car and took a seat part way along the aisle next to Waymier. The two men nodded and muttered a good morning as two strangers might, then sat without speaking. From under his hat brim, Carrick saw several of the other raiders straggle in, finding empty seats here and there. Most of the passengers, friend and stranger alike, had the listless, weary look of early morning.

A few minutes later, the raucous steam whistle ripped the dawn air, and the train jerked into motion.

"We missed it!" Martin Hawkins swore softly as he and John Porter stood on the depot platform, coats and boots in hand, gazing with unbelieving eyes at the smoke disappearing around the bend. "That damned hotel clerk didn't wake us." He and Porter had taken the last room in the hotel, a tiny cubbyhole under the garret, barely big enough for two. He'd failed to tip the clerk, who had failed to give the exhausted men a wake-up call.

"What do we do now?" eighteen year-old Porter asked. His smooth face was pale in the early light.

Hawkins set his boots down beside him, then rubbed his thick mustache, a sinking feeling in his stomach. He had to think quickly and act naturally to avoid arousing any suspicions, and he had to do it confidently to calm the fears of his young companion.

"First, we'll go back inside and finish getting dressed, then we'll figure out something." The truth was, he'd never considered the possibility of missing the train and being left behind by his fellow raiders. "We've got two tickets to Ringgold. We'll just catch the next train north like ordinary civilian passengers."

"I don't want to be around these Rebs," Porter said warily. "We'd best take to the woods and try to escape thataway."

Hawkins slipped on his jacket as he glanced around to make sure no one else was within earshot. "We'll talk it over. But if anyone gets suspicious and starts asking questions, or we get into a tight spot, don't panic. Just let me do the talking. As a last resort, we could always enlist in some Confederate outfit, then wait for a chance to desert and work our way north again."

The look on Porter's face was not one of great confidence.

As the train picked up speed, Carrick's adrenaline began to flow and he found it difficult to sit still. He knew the others, beneath their façades of sleepy indifference, were probably feeling the same thing. Folding his arms across his body, he slouched down in the seat, letting his right hand touch the bone grips of the Remington .36 caliber revolver belted under his corduroy coat. The night before in the hotel room he and the others had cleaned, loaded, and capped their weapons, taking care to keep moisture away from the black powder. The Remington was a comforting presence — but he fervently hoped he'd have no need of it.

The rising sun flickered between the passing trees and stabbed at his eyes through the coach windows as they slid past Marietta. Before they'd run three miles, the sun vanished behind a pewter-colored overcast that hinted of rain.

The door at the end of the coach opened, and the conductor entered. Carrick held his breath and carefully scrutinized the young railroad man who was dressed in a black frock coat, slouch hat, white shirt, and light-colored pants. A gold watch chain was connected to a buttonhole, the other end disappearing into his side pocket. He sported a mustache and small goatee. The conductor swung along the aisle, balancing easily to the sway of the car. Apparently he had no suspicions of anything amiss as he turned right and left, collecting and punching tickets.

Carrick let out his breath in a long sigh when he heard the rear door open and the conductor pass out of the car. Some of the raiders exchanged glances. The first hurdle was past.

The tracks curved to the east in a great circle around the base of Kennesaw Mountain. Carrick gave only a cursory glance at the majestic greening forest of hardwoods that flanked the steep slopes. In an effort to distract himself and calm his nerves, he began to count the number of times the wheels clicked over the rail joints. How much of a fight would they encounter trying to take the train at Big Shanty? As he turned to glance out the window, Josiah Waymier smiled, as if to reassure him everything was going to work out fine. The young man seemed to have no nerves at all.

Five minutes later, the conductor reëntered the car and called out: "Big Shanty! Twenty minutes for breakfast!"

Carrick's heart began to beat faster. As the train slowed to a stop, rows of white tents — Camp McDonald — came into view on the west side of the train. Three weeks before, Andrews had seen a few troops here, but now the fields to the left were one vast encampment — at least four regiments, Carrick estimated. Hundreds of men were coming and going, many of them new recruits in civilian dress.

As soon as the train ground to a halt in a *hiss* of steam, most of the legitimate passengers were on their feet and crowding toward the doors. Through a window, Carrick saw the engineer, fireman, and conductor heading for the Lacy House on the right side of the train.

Carrick had no appetite as he waited tensely for the signal. A minute seemed like twenty as passengers and crew disappeared into the hotel dining room. James Andrews had earlier reëntered the car and was sitting near the door. He rose and nodded toward the raiders' engineer, William Knight, who then followed him out the forward end.

Less than a minute later, Andrews reëntered the coach. In a calm, unhurried voice he said: "Come on, boys. It's all clear. Time to go."

The five passengers who'd remained in the coach barely looked up, apparently suspecting nothing. But in a minute or two it wouldn't matter, Carrick thought, as he rose with the others. They stepped down on the left side of the train.

"Uncouple right here," Andrews said.

Carrick stepped behind the last empty freight car, drew

out the pin, and carefully laid it on the drawbar.

"Climb into the boxcars," Andrews urged in a low voice "Hurry! Get in! Get in!" He waved them forward, for the first time showing the tension he was under. Engineer Knight was already swinging up into the cab of the engine, followed by Alf Wilson, the fireman.

"Get up on the tender and be ready to pass wood," Andrews said to Carrick who needed no urging. He ran forward and Wilson, reaching down, yanked him up by the arm. As Carrick went up the iron ladder and scrambled over the top of the stacked cordwood, he looked down at a sentry who stood only a dozen feet away, casually observing the operation, as if this were routine procedure. Several other soldiers lounged nearby, paying no attention.

The short, blue-eyed Knight stood, hand on throttle, gazing intently at Andrews who grabbed the brass hand rail and stepped up onto the lower step of the engine.

"Go!"

In his haste, Knight threw the valve open too fast. The wheels spun, screeching metal on metal, in a rush of escaping steam. Then the big drivers bit, and the ponderous locomotive lunged forward and began to roll, quickly picking up speed.

"What's for breakfast, George?" Conductor William Fuller inquired as he led the train crew into the dining room of the Lacy House.

"Same as always, Will," the owner replied, looking up from sorting silver change in his cash drawer. "Grits, ham with redeye gravy, eggs, hot biscuits, flapjacks with butter, and coffee."

"Whew! And all for twenty-five cents," Fuller replied, removing his hat to reveal a balding pate, incongruous with his youthful face. "If I ate here every day, I'd weigh three hundred pounds."

The two men smiled at this standard exchange, and Fuller took a seat at his usual table by the curtained front window. He was joined by Jeff Cain, the *General*'s engineer, a frail, consumptive man with a drooping mustache, and Anthony Murphy, a bluff, hearty native of County Wicklow, Ireland, who was foreman of machinery and motive power for the Western & Atlantic Railroad.

"Murphy, you gonna take a look at that new engine they just put into service up at Adairsville?" Fuller said, stirring cream into his coffee.

"Right. I have to decide if the cost of repairs on the old *Turnbull* are worth keeping it in service. Might have to scrap it."

"With the war, I'd say the line needs every engine it can get," Fuller said. "Moving all those troops and food and equipment . . . that's why we're hauling three empty boxcars out there . . . to bring back a lot of bacon from Chattanooga. And, speaking of bacon. . . ." He broke off to sniff the aroma from the plate the waiter had just set before him.

Jeff Cain, the phlegmatic engineer, was digging into a stack of flapjacks, awash in sorghum molasses.

"Jeff, you tie into those pancakes every day, but never gain an ounce," Fuller said.

"It's these lungs," the lean man said, touching his chest. "Can't put any meat on, no matter what I eat."

"Both of us came here by way of Pennsylvania," Murphy put in, "but I understand you moved south for the warmer climate."

"That's a fact," Cain said, wiping his mustache with a napkin. "But it ain't helped much. Reckon I'll have to go some place dry. Too damp in Georgia."

"Yeah, too many days like this," Fuller said, chewing his bacon and toast and gesturing toward the nearby window. "Typical spring day . . . damp and cool. This summer it'll be damp and hot. I believe we're starting to get a little light rain out there right now. And, if I'm any judge, it's setting in for the day." His coffee cup halted halfway to his lips. "What . . . ?" The cup clattered down, sloshing coffee into the saucer.

The two men followed his stare out the window.

"Somebody's stealing our train!"

Gray smoke was huffing from the balloon stack as the big drivers took hold and the front half of the train began to accelerate. Fuller was stunned. For the space of two or three heartbeats, he couldn't grasp the reality of what his eyes were telling him. "By God, they won't get away with it!"

He leaped up, knocking over his chair, and dashed for the door. Cain and Murphy were only a few steps behind. Fuller bounded off the porch and through the gate of the picket fence in time to see the last boxcar disappear around a cut in the low hill. The sound of the locomotive grew dimmer. Smoke hung in the heavy air over the trees to mark its passage.

Fuller paused, frustrated. Cain and Murphy came up, and the three stared at the empty curve of track.

Several soldiers from Camp McDonald ran, shouting, down the track. Two sentries had fired and were reloading their single-shot muskets.

"Who took that train?" Fuller yelled at one of the guards.

"A big man with a full brown beard," came the reply. "He was wearing a dark cape or overcoat."

"Let's go!" Fuller cried.

"On foot?" Murphy sounded incredulous.

"Yeah. That bearded fella got on in Marietta with several men. I'd lay odds they were conscripts for Camp McDonald who don't want to be in the Army."

"What makes you think so?" Murphy asked.

"The camp commander warned me last month to keep an eye out for deserters trying to slip aboard our train. They'll abandon the *General* up the line a ways." With no further discussion, Fuller took off at a dead run along the tracks. In spite of his confident words, he really had little hope of catching the fleeing locomotive. Running after it was his first instinct. At least, it gave physical vent to his frustration and embarrassment at having his train stolen while he looked on helplessly.

"Send a courier back to Marietta!" Murphy yelled at one of the uniformed sentries. "Telegraph a warning up the line that the *General*'s been stolen!" Then he turned and jogged after Fuller, with the consumptive engineer, Cain, limping along in the rear.

"We did it without a fight!" Knight cried. "By God, boys, we're done playing Reb now! We're out-and-out Yankees from here on!" He bounced around the cab, leaning out to watch the encampment and the uncoupled rear of the train slide out of view behind a cutbank.

"Don't get too fired up," Wilson said. He was piling some split oak by his feet near the firebox. "We're not out of the woods yet."

His words proved prophetic. The train's first burst of speed carried them nearly a half mile before the power began to fail. Of its own volition, the *General* ran slower and slower, until it finally came to a stop. Knight was frantically checking everything.

"What's happened?" Andrews demanded.

"Steam's gone down!"

Carrick's stomach felt as if he'd swallowed a lead sinker.

"The fire's almost out!" engineer Knight cried, swinging open the fire door. "Ah, ha! The cylinder cocks are still open," he said, the frown disappearing from his face.

"What?" Carrick asked.

"The crew opened the cocks when they went to breakfast," Fireman Alf Wilson explained, "to allow steam to leak off and prevent water buildup in the cylinders. Water won't compress, and, if it builds up, it could blow the cylinder heads when they start up again." He turned to Knight. "I'll take care of it." He stepped out onto the angle-iron catwalk and worked his way along the hot water jacket to the pilot beam. Then he bent down and closed the cocks on the right side, crossed over the front of the engine and did the same thing on the left.

Knight turned to Carrick. "Let's get some fresh wood and oil on this fire." Then he grabbed the long-nosed oilcan, swung down from the cab, and began "oiling around" as the engineers termed it, making sure all moving parts and journals on the piston rods and drive wheels were properly lubricated.

"While we're stopped, climb that pole and cut the telegraph wire," Andrews yelled at John Scott who had come forward to check the trouble.

Andrews hadn't overlooked anything. Even though there was no telegraph office at Big Shanty, someone might be able to rig up a portable battery, or send a rider back to Marietta to flash a warning ahead up the line.

Scott, lean and agile as a monkey, wrapped his legs around the pole and shinnied up to the crossbar. He knocked off the insulator with the butt of his pistol, grabbed the freed line, and swung down on it, pulling it to the ground. Andrews found a hacksaw in the engine's toolbox, and the tightly stretched wire was quickly severed.

"We got it!" Andrews gloated, rubbing his hands together. "I have a copy of the schedule. Three trains are coming toward us from Chattanooga, but only one of those should prove to be any obstacle. Once we get by it, we'll run full speed, burning the bridges after us." His brown eyes darted here and there and he couldn't suppress a grin. "Now we have those Rebs where we want 'em!"

Carrick had never seen their smooth, calculating leader so excited.

Barely five minutes later, great clouds of black smoke were belching from the stack as oil and wood flamed hot in the firebox. They were under way again, picking up speed and putting Big Shanty farther behind them.

Chapter Five
deception

Amelia Waymier was so angry and frustrated, she didn't know whether to curse or cry. So she did both.

It was the sixth or seventh time during the night the heavy wagon had bogged down. The tired mules couldn't pull the loaded wagon out of the muck that sucked up to the hub of the left rear wheel. Standing to one side, ankle-deep in mud, she held the reins of the animals and wondered what to do next. She was wet through and chilled as the sodden cape hung heavily on her shoulders and back. The brim of her soggy felt hat drooped around her ears.

Through the long black hours, Amelia had been able to keep the team moving at a steady pace on the slick, rutted road. But once, while she was nodding with fatigue, the leaders had nearly plunged into the swollen ford of a stream. At the last second they balked, rearing back. Amelia, suddenly alert, had slammed her foot against the long brake handle. Team and wagon had come to a rattling, skidding halt. After several deep breaths to calm her nerves, Amelia had turned her team away from the rushing water she could hear but not see. Knowing the area, she'd detoured north on a little-used road for two miles around the loop of the normally placid stream.

As the night wore on and rain continued to pour down, the mules had strained to pull the wagon through deep ruts and water-filled holes she couldn't see. Amelia had coaxed and cursed and burned their backsides with the whip. Each time the mules had made the extra effort required to drag the load out of the red clay — until they could pull no more. The wagon had finally become mired in the deep muck.

No wonder this stuff is so good for making bricks, Amelia thought, now realizing that she could actually *see* the color of the mud. She gazed helplessly at the wagon, as gray daylight stole up over the dreary landscape. She murmured a prayer of thanks that at least the rain had stopped as she watched the slow-moving storm draw away to the east.

The six tired mules now stood, heads down, red muck plastered halfway up their sides. The harness and wagon were similarly glopped. She'd been trying to get the team to pull for ten minutes, then realized they had no more left. It was clear she'd have to unload the wagon if they were to get clear. It was the only solution. But did she have the strength? Though only five-foot six and a hundred forty pounds, she'd been used to hard work and, even at the age of fifty-two, fancied herself to be in good physical condition. She thought she could probably do it, if the individual boxes weren't too heavy. But how long would it take her to lighten the wagon sufficiently, pull out, and reload? With dawn breaking, she probably didn't have more than three hours left to reach Cartersville. She didn't know what time the train would stop there, but guessed it would be fairly early in the morning. If she didn't connect with the stolen train, what would she do? Unhitch the mules to fend for themselves, then abandon the wagon? She'd almost forgotten about the alarm that would be raised when the four soldiers she'd flummoxed got to town. The pursuit might be a day or more in coming, but come it would. Escape to the Northern lines would be her only hope. She'd take her own mule that was trailing behind the wagon, and ride away into the hills, carrying one or two of the gold bars. But how would she carry them? Since she generally used her mule to pull a buggy, she'd forgotten to bring a saddle or saddlebags. She had a little cash in the form of gold and silver coins she could use to buy things, but if she started slicing off shavings of gold to purchase necessities, she'd be quickly discovered.

She took a deep breath and exhaled, resigned to the effort of unloading. She needed to focus on success, not failure, she thought as she reached for the wet rope that secured the canvas cover. She had to hurry if she was to make her rendezvous.

The *splatting* of hoofs on the soggy ground startled her. She dragged her boots free of the mud and hurried forward to pull the shotgun from under the wagon seat. She'd hardly eared back both hammers when a black-topped buggy, pulled by a single horse, came around the bend from behind her.

"Whoa!" The driver pulled up a few yards away, his eyes narrowing at the double-barreled weapon she held in the crook of her arm. He pushed back his hat, and she could see his face clearly in the pearling light. "What's the trouble?" he called. He was a heavy-set man about her own age, she guessed, and sported a short, graying beard. She noted he wore a belted pistol holster, but made no move toward it.

"Bogged down," she said, nodding toward the wagon. "Mules have about give out," she continued, falling into the vernacular of the region.

The man looped the reins around an iron rod on the

dashboard and climbed out. "I'll give you a hand. Maybe we can get it free." He brushed past the lowered shotgun to survey the mired wheel. "You sure got 'er in there, right enough. There ain't no bottom to some o' these roads in the spring. You must be haulin' a right heavy load." He turned toward her.

"It's heavy," she agreed. "We . . . me and the mules . . . been at it most of the night. They just plumb wore down. Can't pull it out."

"Then it looks to me like we'll have to unload it," the stranger said, confirming what she'd already decided. "By the way, my name's Barney Leathers." He swept off his hat to reveal thinning gray hair.

She eased down the hammers of the shotgun, and took his outstretched hand. "Good to know you. I'm . . . Jane Segal," she lied, in case he might recognize the name Waymier, or in the unlikely event word of the bullion theft had somehow gotten ahead of her.

He nodded, and put his hat back on. "Let's get to it. I've got to be to work in about two hours."

"What kind of work?" Amelia inquired as the man's thick fingers worked at the wet knots.

"I'm the keeper of the Cass wood and water station just north of Cartersville," he replied, flinging back the wet canvas, then removing the pegs to drop the tailgate.

Her heart gave a leap. "Where all the trains stop?"

"Sure is," he said with a hint of pride. "It's just one of several up and down the Georgia line. We're spaced far enough apart so the locomotives can get fuel and water when they need it."

"So any trains coming north out of Atlanta would have to stop at Cass station?" she asked as if making polite conversation.

"Right you are. Even if they pulled an extra tender full of wood, they'd still have to take on water there."

"That's where I'm headed," she said, seeing that he was eyeing the bold stenciling on the sides of the wooden crates.

He appeared not to hear as he yanked one of the boxes toward him by its rope handle. "Uh! Heavy. Does that mean what it says?" he asked, jabbing a finger at the lettering.

"Yes," she replied, her heart pounding. "I'm taking that Gatling gun ammunition to a northbound train so it can help re-supply the troops at Chattanooga.

Leathers paused and gave her a closer scrutiny. She held her breath. Not being an accomplished liar, she hoped the dim early light would conceal her nervousness.

"How come you happen to be haulin' military ordnance?" he finally asked, swinging the box off the tailgate and setting it down a few feet away on solid ground.

"It didn't start out that way. Three of the home guard were escorting it to the train, but they were old men and couldn't stand traveling and sleeping in the constant wet. They took sick about the time they were passing my house some twenty miles back." The prevarication blossomed on her lips as if she'd been cultivating it all her life. "They had a train to meet, so I volunteered to take it the last few miles for 'em."

"No other men around?" he asked suspiciously.

"No. My husband's dead, and all the younger men are off to fight. Besides, my house is out in the country, and I didn't have time to go hunting any men. Reckon I could do as well as most of them, even if I was to find one or two willing to go."

"Did they give you any written orders or authorization papers to prove what you're telling me?" Leathers asked, without pausing in his work of unloading.

"Nope. Didn't think I'd need any just to travel twenty miles. The main thing was to get this load to the upbound train from Atlanta to Chattanooga sometime this morning," she said sharply, hoping the exasperation in her voice would cut off further questions. As if to dismiss his suspicions, she waded back into the mud and began helping unload.

"Think I'll just have a look-see into one of these crates," Leathers said, straightening up and pulling out a large sheath knife to pry off one of the lids.

Amelia felt a sudden panic and sneaked a quick look at the shotgun leaning against the front wheel. If he somehow got the lid open, she'd have to feign ignorance of the bullion. But she eased herself toward the gun, just in case.

"I wouldn't open that if I was you," she said, trying to keep her voice from shaking. Then she noticed the leaded tin strips through the hasps and padlocks. "You'd be in a lot of trouble if you was to break them government seals."

He hesitated, knife in hand. Finally he shoved the thick blade back into its sheath. "Your tale sounds a mite fishy to me," he said. " But I reckon it's so far-fetched, it might just be the truth." He resumed swinging the cases off the tailgate without further conversation.

Amelia struggled to lift the boxes off the waist-high wagon bed. Each of the crates must have weighed at least sixty pounds. She tried to take some of the load on a hip, but caught her breath as the sharp edges and corners dug into her flesh. Finally she crawled up into the wagon and shoved the boxes toward the tailgate for Leathers to hand down.

Thirty minutes later they both sank down, panting. A stack of nearly three dozen crates was piled on the ground.

"That's about half of them," Leathers said. "Let's give

'er a try now." He took his knife and hacked some branches off a small nearby cedar tree, then stuffed the evergreens down in front of the rear wheel.

She picked up the reins while he walked around to the front and took hold of the both leaders' bridles. "Ready?" he called.

"Yep."

"Pop that whip and let's go!"

She shook the long, braided whip out of its coil and swung it overhead. The lash snaked out, popping near the ears of the wheelers.

"Hyah! Giddap, mules! Go! Pull!"

The team lunged forward as one, straining, churning the stiffening mud. Leathers pulled forward on the harness, yelling, urging.

Slowly, agonizingly the wagon began to move, the wheel sucking loose from its prison. Then the big wheels turned a full revolution as the animals got purchase, and the wagon came up out of the mud and rolled several feet onto solid ground, streaming brown water.

"Whoa!" Leathers came around to one side. "Now let's get you loaded up and out of here. Follow me the last three miles to Cass station. Both of us have a train to meet."

Chapter Six

aboard the general

"Moon's Station coming up," Josiah Waymier said.

"What's Moon's Station?" J. J. Andrews asked.

"Just a siding and a shed for the use of a section gang."

While the train had been halted to close the cocks and cut the telegraph, Andrews had brought Josiah Waymier to the cab of the locomotive. Carrick assumed it was because Waymier's knowledge of the road was needed up front. The men in the boxcars had been instructed to close the doors and remain quiet.

"Slow down and stop," Andrews said calmly as they approached the siding.

Knight looked surprised, but did as he was told without question.

A group of bronzed men in overalls leaned on their pry bars and mallets and turned to stare at them. Apparently they were as surprised by the faces of the strange train crew as they were by the unscheduled stop.

"You're about twenty minutes early," a burly man said, stepping forward, as Andrews swung down from the cab. "And where's Jeff Cain?"

"This is a special run. We're taking a load of ammunition through to General Beauregard in Chattanooga. I'm

J. J. Andrews, an official of the Western and Atlantic."

The big man held out a beefy hand as he eyed the well-dressed Andrews. "I'm Jackson Bond, foreman of this here section crew. What can I do for you?"

"We could use some tools to repair any damaged track along the way. We left in such a hurry, we didn't have time to load any."

"Well, we got only about what we need for our own men. . . ." He paused, and looked around. "Here's a crowbar you can have. Will that help?"

"If that's all you can spare, we'll take it," Andrews said, accepting the bar with one hand and shaking Bond's hand with the other. "And we're mighty grateful for your help. It's little things like this that sometimes decide great battles."

With that he climbed aboard, and Knight put the *General* into motion.

"You can open 'er up some now, Mister Andrews," Waymier said a couple of minutes later. "We're on a fairly straight downgrade for the next six miles to Acworth."

The leader nodded to Knight who eased the throttle open. They picked up speed — to fifty, then to sixty and beyond, the reciprocating pistons pumping the long rods faster and faster, whirling the big iron drive wheels. Each revolution carried them farther ahead of any possible pursuit.

The *General* rocked and swayed, jerking the tender from side to side so violently that Carrick threw himself onto the rough woodpile to keep from being pitched off. The speed took his breath as the bushes along the right-of-way flashed past in a pale green blur. He gripped his hat in one fist while his hair whipped in the wind and his eyes watered from the stinging wood smoke.

Alf Wilson was yelling something at him.

"What?" Carrick cupped a hand behind his ear.

"More wood!"

Carrick jammed his hat back on his head, braced his knees widely to free both hands, and began shoving down the hunks of split cordwood to Wilson. Protecting his hands with the fireman's heavy gloves, Wilson flung open the firebox door and heaved the wood into the flames.

Andrews said something to Knight, and the engineer eased back on the throttle. The *General* gradually slowed until they were doing only about twenty-five miles per hour.

Carrick paused in his wood passing and sat down on the pile to catch his breath. After several miles at such a frightening speed, he felt as if they were proceeding barely faster than a horse could walk. Was something wrong with the engine?

Waymier was seated on the left side of the cab, watching out the forward window. "Acworth a mile ahead," he announced.

"Stop here," Andrews said.

Knight applied the brakes, and the *General* slowed to a halt.

"Let's cut the telegraph line again and this time make sure it can't be reconnected without a lot of work," Andrews said, directing Scott up the nearest pole with the hacksaw.

"Mister Andrews, there's a stack of cross-ties over here!" one of the men yelled from the open door of a boxcar. "We could throw 'em on the tracks to slow down anybody behind us."

"Good idea. Go to it."

Men spilled out of the boxcars, eager for some action. With one person on each end of a tie, the men worked like a swarm of ants, moving the stack of wood. In less than ten minutes, more than forty ties obstructed the tracks for a hundred yards.

At the same time, Scott had placed his feet in the hands of two strong men and been hoisted up the pole, cut the wire with the saw, and dropped the severed end of the wire to the ground. Then he jumped down, and Andrews directed him to fasten the loose end to the undercarriage of the last boxcar.

"There she is . . . several turns and a clove hitch," Scott said, crawling out from under.

"Let's go, men!" Andrews yelled, and the raiders swarmed back into the boxcars.

With a *whoof! whoof!*, the *General* got under way. The telegraph wire grew taut and snapped loose from the insulator, then snagged on the crosstree of the next pole, jerking it over, dragging it into the next pole, and the next. As the train accelerated, four more poles were pulled down before the line finally snapped.

"They shouldn't make their wire so strong," Andrews commented to the men in the cab.

The faces relaxed into laughter, and Carrick felt his tension ease as he joined in with the rest. He realized he could never do what Andrews was doing. Carrick knew himself to be a practical man who always applied his best efforts to the task at hand, but he was not a planner or a strategist. He excelled at making quick, on-the-spot decisions. If he thought too much about the larger picture, he tended to become overwhelmed and sometimes depressed by the complexity or enormity of a problem.

At Andrews's command, the men closed the boxcar doors to conceal themselves. They rolled right through the village of Acworth without slowing down and proceeded a few more miles to Allatoona. As the buildings flashed by, Carrick and the others in the cab ignored the small group of people on the depot platform. Just beyond Allatoona, the train passed through a deep cut in a hill as they steamed northward, feeling more confident with every passing mile.

After another two miles, Andrews again ordered a halt in the deserted countryside. "Tear up a rail behind us." The bearded leader climbed down, Knight set the brakes on the engine, and all hands went to help. But, without the proper tools, the job proved more difficult than expected. They had no pry bar with a curved notch on one end for pulling spikes. But they made do without one as they wedged and battered out a few spikes with the crowbar. The men worked without talking. The clanking of iron against iron punctuated the sounds of their labored breathing.

Carrick squeezed in beside five others, squatted, and gripped the free end of the rail. "On three. Ready? One, two, *three!*" They heaved upward in unison, straining every muscle. With a screech of protest, the remaining spikes pulled out of the dry wood and the rail came loose.

"Pitch it in the car and let's be off!" Andrews yelled.

The job had taken nearly ten minutes, but Carrick sensed no panic. They had a good head start.

Just before they climbed into the cab, Knight borrowed a red bandanna from Andrews and tied it to a stick on the front of the engine. "Signals to any train we meet that there's another one following behind us," he explained as he swung his compact frame up by the hand rails. "It'll make any southbound trains we pass stay on the sidings a little longer."

"Don't run too fast," Andrews cautioned as Knight opened the throttle, and the engine began huffing. "Keep to the schedule so we won't arouse suspicion. And that way we'll also meet oncoming trains at the right place for them to pull onto the sidings and let us pass."

The five men in the cab grinned at each other. Carrick shared the confidence of success they all felt.

Chapter Seven
on foot and pole car

Conductor William Fuller considered himself to be in good physical condition but, with pounding heart and limber legs, he was forced to slacken his pace to a walk every few hundred yards as he pursued the train. Sucking in great lungs full of the cool, damp air, he came to the realization he'd not been very active since being promoted from brakeman. In spite of his physical distress, his determination had not flagged. By God, he was going to chase his train until he caught those thieves, or died trying. The last two and a half miles to Moon's Station he covered in a staggering run on legs that were beginning to feel like wooden stumps.

"They stole the *General*!" he gasped.

Jackson Bond, foreman of the section gang, looked up from directing men onto pole cars. Everyone crowded around Fuller as he faltered to a stop, hands on knees, sweat dripping from his face. He couldn't speak another word for several seconds. *This is what the first marathon runner must have felt like just before he shouted "Victory" and dropped dead from exhaustion,* Fuller thought.

"What happened?"

"What'd he say?"

"Stand back and give him air. Something's bad wrong."

"Here, Mister Fuller. Come, sit down." Jackson Bond took him by the arm and led him to a seat on a stack of ties.

It was a full two minutes before Fuller was able to gasp: "Somebody . . . stole . . . the *General*!"

"By God!" Jackson Bond cried. "Those sons-of-bitches stopped and asked us for some tools."

"Hope you . . . didn't give 'em . . . any!" Fuller panted.

"Only one crowbar. We had to keep the rest for our own work."

Fuller nodded, mopping his baldpate and face with a large blue bandanna. His clothes felt damp and heavy from sweat and the misty rain.

"How . . . long ago?"

"Maybe three quarters of an hour."

"There's two more!" one of the men said, pointing.

Fuller looked up to see the figures of Murphy and Cain coming toward them. From all appearances, they were pretty well spent. By the time the two men approached, Fuller's breathing had steadied.

"They stopped here about forty-five minutes ago."

"You going to keep after 'em?" Murphy panted as he came up.

"Yeh."

Murphy turned to Bond. "Then we're taking one of your pole cars."

"I'll come along and help."

Fuller nodded, glad the muscular foreman was volunteering.

"This is the best one," Bond said, guiding them to a pole car. The four of them — Fuller, Bond, Murphy, and Cain piled aboard.

The bearings were well greased and the car rolled easily

as Fuller and Bond took the first shift, sitting on each side, and pushing with one leg. Every half mile or so, they switched sides to push with the other leg. Meanwhile, Murphy and Cain, stationed at the back corners of the car, were pushing with two stout poles.

They made good time until a half mile out of Acworth. Here they were forced to stop and clear the track of about four dozen cross-ties and a tangle of telegraph lines and poles.

"I don't think these men are deserting conscripts," Murphy grunted, dragging a tie out of the way. "They're too serious about escaping."

"I'm thinking the same thing," Fuller said as they finally climbed back aboard. "These must be Federal men."

Fuller was relieved when they rolled into Acworth, and recruited more help. Several men grabbed their guns and eagerly piled onto the car until there was no room left for others waiting to get aboard. Someone shoved two double-barreled shotguns at Murphy and Fuller. In a matter of minutes, they were moving north again toward Allatoona, with strong, rested men propelling the car with poles.

Looking back, Fuller saw another pole car had been appropriated. It was filled with the overflow of men who were hot to join the chase.

Two miles farther, they were rolling down a long grade at ten or twelve miles an hour.

"Look out!" Bond yelled. "Missing rail!" The four men now pushing tried to brake with their poles, but too late. The right side wheels hit the gap, plowed into ballast and cross-ties and flipped the car. The men were pitched off down a grassy slope in a tangle of flailing arms and legs. A shot cracked as a cocked weapon discharged.

"Son-of-a-bitch!"

Cursing and grumbling filled the air as the men clambered to their feet, checking for broken bones and bruises. The bullet had not struck anyone.

The men riding the second car saw the wreck in time to stop.

It took only a minute for the many willing hands to lift and carry the cars forward around the break.

"Keep a sharp look-out ahead!" Fuller called, rubbing a painful knot on his forehead. "These damn' Yanks think they've slowed us down, but they'll have to do more than that!" Fuller was already thinking ahead to the bridge over the Etowah River. If the fleeing raiders had a long enough lead to stop and fire the bridge, he and the rest of the pursuers would have to swim the cold river or fashion some kind of boat. If the bridge was burning but was still intact, they could cross the remaining superstructure on foot. Once on the other side, maybe they could commandeer a locomotive at the town of Cartersville and continue the pursuit. With his jaw set, he stared grimly ahead along the tracks. He had armed reinforcements now and would stay after the thieves with every means possible — until stopped, or the raiders made good their escape.

Chapter Eight
unexpected cargo

Engineer Knight slowed the *General* as it rounded a long curve, then eased the locomotive up onto the approach to the Etowah River bridge. Carrick looked down through the triangulated trusses that were flicking past. The massive stone abutments that held them high above the water looked solid enough to last for another two hundred years. The bolted wooden beams were another matter, he thought, as they creaked and groaned with the passage of the train. The river, thirty feet below, was swollen by the spring rains and swirling with driftwood. The *General* chuffed slowly across and onto solid ground again.

"Damn!" Andrews swore softly as they came in sight of a locomotive standing on a siding only a few yards away. The smoke issuing from the stack showed that it had steam up and was ready for work. "Where did that come from?"

"It's the *Yonah,*" Josiah Waymier said. "A privately owned locomotive that's used to run up that spur about five miles to the Cooper Iron Works."

"Shall we shoot a few holes in its boiler?" Alf Wilson asked.

"No. Too many men around. It would provoke a fight," Andrews said. "So far, we've gotten by with deception.

We'll use guile as long as we can. There's no reason for them to suspect us or come after us."

"What about firing that bridge?" Carrick asked. "That would surely put a stop to anyone following."

Andrews looked back at the bridge, and shook his head sadly. "Timbers are too wet. The only fuel we have is that can of oil for the engine. By the time we gathered enough dry brush to get a good blaze going, those men would see what we're up to and we'd have a battle on our hands. We'd best get on up the line and try another bridge that's more isolated."

The *General* continued to steam slowly past the town of Cartersville without stopping. Carrick smiled at the looks of surprise and consternation on the faces of the passengers waiting on the depot platform. *Figuring we're a freight instead of the passenger train they were expecting,* he thought.

Just as they passed the depot, the clock in the tower of the courthouse a block up the hill began to strike. Carrick glanced up from his seat atop the tender and saw the hands pointing at 7:45. The sun should have been up and shining warmly overhead by now, but the overcast and misty drizzle persisted. Andrews was right about trying to fire the ten-by-ten timbers of the Etowah bridge: without a lot of fuel and time, it wouldn't have been possible.

Cartersville was soon left behind, and Andrews ordered Knight to hold at a steady twenty miles an hour because they would be stopping in two miles at the Cass wood and water station.

"Let me do the talking, boys," Andrews cautioned them as the water tower drew closer. Knight applied the brakes so as to bring the *General* to a stop directly under the waterspout of the trackside tank. "Where are those wood passes?"

Knight got up and raised the hinged seat cover. "Right here. First thing I checked when we got aboard. Glad the other engineer didn't carry them in his overalls. Without these, we'd have to requisition wood at gunpoint."

Carrick knew that engineers were supplied with passes to be handed over for each cord of wood taken aboard. This way, the efficiency of each locomotive on the road could be calculated, and, if an engineer wasted wood or lost his passes, money was deducted from his pay.

The *General* ground to a halt in a hiss of steam, and Carrick, Alf Wilson, and Waymier jumped down and began to load wood that was stacked in cords nearby. A balding man with a beard approached and took the passes Andrews handed him.

"I'm Barney Leathers," the man said, extending his hand. "You're about a half hour early. And where's Jeff Cain and the regular crew?"

"J. J. Andrews." The two men shook hands. "I'm an official of the Western and Atlantic and the government has authorized me to load a train with powder and ball and run it through to General Beauregard as fast as possible."

Leathers nodded. "I heard about Shiloh. Guess they'll have one helluva fight on their hands as they pull back from there."

Carrick watched out of the corner of his eye as he took the wood from Wilson and handed it to Waymier who pitched it up into the tender. He sensed that Leathers was impressed by the commanding presence of Andrews.

"By God, if Beauregard needs it, I'd give him the shirt off my back, too," Leathers said. "Here, you can even have my copy of the schedule of the road from here north. That should help you avoid any delays."

"Much obliged."

"I guess I shouldn't have doubted your story, Missus Segal," Leathers added, turning to an approaching older woman. "This lady has a wagonload of Gatling gun ammunition to add to your train."

The self-assured look disappeared from Andrews's face, and he opened his mouth to make some excuse or objection. But, before he could speak, Josiah Waymier looked up and dropped the log of firewood he was passing. "Ma!" he cried. Heads turned in confusion, and the wood passing halted.

Atop the engine, Knight held the counterbalanced spout that was gushing water into the boiler and apparently didn't hear the exchange going on below.

"What?" Leathers looked from one to another. "You know this woman?"

"I ought to," Waymier replied. "That's my mother, Amelia."

"Josiah!" Amelia rushed forward and flung herself at her son, embracing him. Carrick saw her whisper something in his ear. They backed away at arm's length.

"Ma, what are you doing here? I never expected to see you."

"Mister Leathers knows all about it. I'll explain later," she said. "Let's get this ammunition aboard. General Beauregard's waiting for it."

Carrick could almost see Andrews's mind racing. They couldn't open the doors of the boxcars without revealing the armed raiders in each one. Yet, Andrews dared not refuse the ammunition without arousing suspicion.

Leathers was outnumbered, but Carrick didn't think Andrews was ready to tip his hand just yet, even though he saw the leader casually brush back his cape to reveal the butt of his holstered pistol as he said: "I'm not sure we have room for that wagonload of cartridges. We weren't expecting it."

"Surely you can cram it in somewhere," Leathers said. "A Gatling gun is a mighty fearsome weapon. Worth a whole company of infantry. It can put the fear of God into those Yanks. It'd be a shame if Beauregard didn't have the use of it."

"Where's the load?" Andrews asked.

"Right over there in my wagon," Amelia said. "Seventy-two wooden crates."

"Bring it around to the other side of the train. I might be able to fit it into the first boxcar." Andrews had backed up to the side of the car and was speaking loudly, apparently to warn the men listening inside. He reached into his vest pocket and drew out a ten-dollar gold eagle. "Mister Leathers, while a couple of my men are helping her, would you be so kind as to fill in here and give us a hand loading this wood? Time is of the essence."

Leathers took the coin. "Be glad to." He fell to with Alf Wilson, pitching the cordwood up into the tender. "Since you're running off schedule, you'd best go slow and keep a flagman out ahead to prevent a collision on one o' those blind curves."

"Right." Andrews nodded.

Amelia Waymier drove the mules and wagon across the track in front of the locomotive and down alongside the train, out of Leathers's sight. Andrews stayed to help with the wooding while Carrick and Waymier crawled under a boxcar to assist.

Josiah rapped softly on the door of the car with a prearranged signal. Carrick could hear Andrews talking loudly to Leathers to mask any sounds coming from the men inside the car.

The raiders inside slid open the door about four feet,

and Waymier whispered what they were about. The wagon bed was nearly the same level as the floor of the car. So, with several willing hands working quickly, the wooden cases were slid across and shoved back out of sight. While they worked, Amelia stood watch from the wagon seat, ready to give warning if Leathers should start toward their side of the train.

"Hurry. Here he comes," Amelia hissed twenty minutes later.

The last two boxes were shoved inside, and the door slid shut just as Leathers rounded the rear of the last boxcar. Andrews was one step behind, still talking to distract him.

"Ah, looks like you had room, after all," Leathers said, looking at the empty wagon.

"Had to do some shifting around, but we got it all in," Carrick said.

"Well, you've got two more cords of wood aboard, so you're set to go," Leathers said.

"Thanks for your help, Mister Leathers," Andrews said, pumping his hand. "Get aboard, boys!" he yelled. "We've got to make some time."

Carrick looked at Amelia Waymier who was still sitting on the wagon seat, reins in hand. For the first time, he noticed how mud-spattered the animals and wagon were. Josiah vaulted out of the wagon and gave his mother a hand down.

"Mister Leathers, I'm going with them," she announced.

The stationkeeper looked startled.

"I've got kin up the line," she explained before he could reply. "Just keep the team and wagon until someone comes for them. That extra mule is mine, but you can have him for being so kind. Hadn't been for you I wouldn't have made it here on time."

"But. . . ."

"I'm taking my shotgun, this carbine, and my extra clothes. Someone will come for the wagon and team."

As she spoke, she was handing her son the Spencer and shotgun and retrieving her gunny sack of clothing. She moved toward the steps of the locomotive. "Might be a good idea to stand those mules under the waterspout and give 'em a good wash down. The wagon, too. Just turn 'em out to graze. Won't cost you nothin' for grain."

"But, I . . . ," Leathers started to object at this unexpected development.

She swung herself up into the cab, and Carrick climbed the ladder to the top of the tender.

Knight eased out the throttle, the wheels slipped, bit, and they were under way.

Carrick let out a long breath. Thanks to some quick thinking, they'd passed another obstacle.

As the train picked up speed, Carrick could see Mrs. Waymier talking to her son and Andrews with animated gestures, but, because of the engine and wind noise, he couldn't hear what was being said.

Suddenly Andrews threw up his hands and whooped a great laugh. A huge grin split his face above the beard. More conversation followed, and Carrick saw Alf Wilson and Knight shaking their heads in wonder.

Finally Josiah climbed the ladder to the tender and said: "Those men in the boxcars don't know what they're sitting on back there." Then he proceeded to relate a tale of deception, treachery, and theft of gold bullion, with his mother as the main actor in the drama.

Carrick was dumbfounded and threw a glance down into the cab at Amelia Waymier, a graying, older woman. "Damn! Looks are sure deceiving," he said. "For sheer nerve and grit, it beats anything we've done so far," he said. "You come from mighty good stock," he said to Josiah who was wearing a semi-permanent grin affixed to his lean face. Then Carrick grew serious. "What will happen to her if we're caught? Do you really have relatives up toward Chattanooga where she's going to get off?"

"Naw! That was just talk for the station man's sake. If she can steal a load of gold from four Reb soldiers, she can face anything *we* can," he said proudly.

"No doubt about it, but I'd sure hate to see her get hurt or killed if we get into a tight spot and have to shoot our way out."

"Let's have some more wood down here!" Alf Wilson yelled up at them.

The train arrived at Kingston at 8:30, slightly ahead of schedule.

"The freights we have to pass haven't arrived yet," Andrews said. "But there's the passenger train from Rome."

As the *General* ground to a stop, just to the right of the station, Andrews swung down and quickly went into his guise of railroad executive. The stationmaster came out to meet him, and he repeated his cover story about taking a special trainload of powder to General Beauregard, who was short of ammunition following the battle at Shiloh. "Have to run this through to Corinth, Mississippi, as quick as we can," Andrews concluded. "I'm sure the regular passenger and mail train will be along shortly from Atlanta."

Carrick had descended from the cab and stood by the locomotive, waiting for Andrews and ready to give the alarm to the men hidden in the boxcars if anything went wrong. In order to prevent any questions about a woman in the cab, Andrews had instructed Amelia to put her hair up under her man's felt hat and to sit on the right side of the engine, away from the depot. She was still wearing her mud-spattered man's clothing.

Several passengers from Rome were waiting on the platform to transfer to the upbound train.

"Why didn't the superintendent of the road send some word ahead about a special train?" one of them asked.

"I can't speak for the superintendent," Andrews replied.

"Helluva way to run a railroad, interrupting service like that," another man grumbled. "And how come the telegraph line is down south of here?"

"That's the *General,* right enough," another remarked, "the same locomotive that always pulls the morning passenger train. But I don't know none o' them fellas on board her."

"And, lookee there . . . they're not even trailing a caboose."

"Whole thing looks a little fishy to me."

Andrews ignored the waiting passengers as he continued talking to the stationmaster.

"There's a southbound freight due in here any minute," the stationmaster said.

"I know. Give me your keys to the switch and I'll have my engineer back 'er down on a siding to wait."

Andrews took the keys and stepped up onto the lower step of the engine. "Pull ahead a quarter mile."

Carrick stayed where he was and watched the locomotive slowly steam away, pulling the cars. He had an uneasy sense of being left behind in the midst of the enemy, and wondered briefly what had happened to Porter and Hawkins who had somehow missed the train.

Carrick tried to look nonchalant as he watched the distant figure of Andrews shifting the throw rod of the switch to the turnout position. The *General* backed its tender and three boxcars onto the siding parallel and to the right of the mainline.

Then began a nerve-straining wait for the down freight. Agonizing minutes dragged. There was nothing to do. Josiah and Amelia Waymier climbed down to stretch their legs. Engineer Knight and Fireman Alf Wilson stayed in the cab.

Carrick saw a Confederate officer approach Andrews. The two of them spoke for a moment, then approached the train. "Boys," Andrews said quietly, "this is Allen Clark. Don't be fooled by the uniform. He's a Union man . . . an old friend who's a Federal undercover man like me."

Clark touched the brim of his hat as his gaze stopped on Amelia Waymier.

"It's a long story, Allen," Andrews said, at his friend's questioning look. "I'll fill you in later."

"Mister Clark, it's a pleasure to meet you," Amelia said, her tired eyes brightening as she extended her hand.

"It's Allen, ma'am," he replied, starting to raise her fingers to his lips, then stopped, apparently realizing she was in male disguise. "Good luck to all of you," Clark said, his intense blue eyes scanning them. "I'd better get back to the depot before anyone gets suspicious." He nodded, and moved away.

About ten minutes later, the whistle of a locomotive was heard and a downward bound freight rumbled into view around a bend, slowing and coming to a halt at the station platform.

The engine bore a red flag in front, indicating another train was following. Andrews approached the conductor and asked him to move on down a few hundred yards to make room so the next freight wouldn't block the switch.

The engineer complied with the request, and then the waiting began again.

When the strain became almost unbearable, Carrick approached the leader. "Shall I tell the men what's going on?" he asked.

"Yes."

Carrick sauntered alongside the last car. Pausing at the door, he said quietly: "Boys, we have to wait for another southbound freight. It's a little behind time and the folks around here are getting uneasy and suspicious. Just relax, but stay ready for anything."

He moved ahead and gave the same message to the men hidden in the other two boxcars, pretending to check the wheels and journal boxes as he did so. He could hear a slight stirring inside and added: "Be as still as you can. Everything is OK for now."

Carrick moved on and climbed up into the cab. Knight was outside, checking the piston rods and all the connections. He climbed back up and pulled out his watch.

"Nothing to do but wait," Carrick said.

"Yes, there is," the engineer said. "I'll have to run this engine slowly up and down the siding if we're here a few more minutes."

"Why?"

"Got to keep the furnace crown sheet covered with water."

Carrick gave him a blank look.

"A feed water pump is driven by one of the piston rods," Fireman Wilson explained. "We have to be moving to make it work."

Carrick nodded, thinking he had a lot to learn about steam engines.

The grueling wait stretched out and the delay continued.

How much longer could they keep up this charade? In spite of the cool morning, Carrick began to perspire. His empty stomach was cramping with hunger and nervousness. He couldn't stop fidgeting, but hoped his tension wasn't being communicated to the others in the cab.

They were losing all the valuable time they had gained earlier. If anyone *was* pursuing them, they would have a good chance to catch up while the *General* sat on a siding.

Chapter Nine
by steam and shank's mare

By the time the lead pole car approached the Etowah River bridge, Conductor William Fuller had regained his wind and his strength. He was relieved to see the bridge intact and evidently undamaged.

"By God, we're in luck, boys!" Fuller cried, as they rolled across. "There's the *Yonah*. It hasn't left for the iron-works yet."

As they cleared the bridge, Cain said: "They're reversing it."

Fuller jumped off before the pole car came to a stop. "Hold up a minute!" he yelled at the men who were heaving at the turntable. He ran over and quickly filled them in on the situation.

"They passed here hardly an hour and a half ago," one of the trainmen said. "We were waitin' on our coal ship-ment."

"Forget about the coal for now," Murphy said. "We're taking the *Yonah* to go after them. I'll be responsible for re-imbursing the ironworks for the use of it."

The section hands jumped off to help push the little turntable, one too small for both the locomotive and tender. First one, and then the other, had to be wrenched around by muscle power.

"Whew! When did they last grease this thing?" Bond grunted as he and his men strained to rotate the turntable.

Finally the tender was coupled to the engine, but it was facing south instead of north. "Forget it. We haven't got time to turn it around," Fuller said. "Hey, you men!" he yelled at six Confederate soldiers waiting for a southbound train "Get aboard if you want to come with us." The soldiers, eager for the chase, clambered onto the flatcar being coupled to the tender. Spikes, tools, and some sections of extra rail were heaved onto the car.

In fifteen minutes, the engineer of the *Yonah* opened the throttle and they were off, pushing the coal tender and flatcar ahead of them.

Fuller and Murphy stationed themselves at the brake wheel on the forward end of the flatcar to watch for obstructions or broken rails.

"Damn' shame there's no telegraph at Cartersville," Murphy remarked as they rolled past the depot and began gaining speed.

"We've got to cut down their lead," Fuller said. His stomach tensing at the order he had to give, he picked his way over the piles of rails and gear toward the tender and yelled at the engineer: "Give 'er all the steam you've got!"

The engineer nodded. Sitting sideways in his seat to watch where he was going, he eased the throttle handle open, and the old *Yonah* began to roll. Faster and faster the train steamed in reverse. Cartersville disappeared among the hills behind them as they leveled out onto forested terrain.

A misty rain whipped over them, and Fuller faced away from it as he pulled out his pocket watch — 9:45.

As their speed rose past fifty, the car began jerking and

swaying, wheel flanges screeching against the rails. He almost regretted giving the engineer a free hand. It would be disastrous if they came upon another gap in the rails. They would never be able to stop quickly enough, but, if they were going to catch the *General*, they had to take the chance. The Yankees had passed through Cartersville ninety minutes ahead of them. And it had taken fifteen more minutes to get the *Yonah* coupled to the two cars and under way. Fuller groaned inwardly. Their only hope of catching the raiders would be if the stolen train had a breakdown or was delayed by southbound traffic. Fuller knew the track was not clear all the way. The stolen train *would* be delayed. The thieves would have to keep to the road's regular schedule if they were to meet and pass opposing trains at the proper sidings. His spirits perked up.

Wood ties flashed under their wheels in a blur, and he looked away from the oncoming track to avoid becoming dizzy.

Kingston came into view ahead. It seemed incredible they could be there already. Crouching next to Murphy and Cain at the end of the flatcar, Fuller again consulted his watch, and whistled softly. Thirteen miles in fifteen minutes. They were really moving.

The *Yonah* slowed and ground to a halt, hissing steam, only a few yards from the cowcatcher of another locomotive. They were still more than a quarter mile from the depot. Fuller, Murphy, and Cain jumped off, along with the half dozen soldiers, and ran ahead.

"Two southbound freights, end to end!" Fuller panted as they dashed toward the depot.

Murphy nodded, then veered off and headed straight toward the nearby locomotive, *New York*, shouting orders at the train crew as he went.

"When did the *General* leave?" Fuller yelled, bounding up onto the depot platform.

The stationmaster looked startled. "Twenty-two minutes ago," he replied, glancing back inside at the wall regulator. "They were delayed a good hour, waiting for those downbound freights."

"Good!" Fuller said with an elated grin. "We're hot on their tail."

"What?"

"Those were Yankee raiders who stole that train."

All the waiting passengers burst into excited talk.

"Get on that telegraph key and wire a warning ahead to Adairsville and Dalton."

"Can't. Just tried to send a routine message, and the line's dead."

"We could send a man ahead on horseback," Cain suggested.

"Not fast enough. Let's just keep after 'em by train."

Fuller and Cain jumped off the platform, followed by several men shouting threats of death and torture at the absent Yankees.

"Don't waste time trying to move those trains," Fuller told Cain. "Just take another one. There! The *William R. Smith* has just come in from Rome. Throw the switch so we can clear it onto the main line."

Oliver Hardin, an engineer Fuller knew, manned the controls of the Rome engine. Fuller vaulted onto the lower step of the cab and told him the situation. "It's urgent we take this train to catch them."

"I'm ready," Hardin said, leaning on the window armrest.

"I'll uncouple the passenger coach and signal you when to pull out."

Word of the theft had spread, and, as Fuller pulled the pin, men scrambled out of the detached passenger coach and ran ahead to get aboard the baggage car.

Fuller stepped out from between the cars and waved to Hardin. The *William R. Smith* began to move, pulling only its tender and one baggage car.

As the train gathered speed, Murphy yelled — "Hey, wait!" — waving his arms and running across the tracks toward them.

Bystanders were piling into the open side door of the baggage car as the train cleared the switch and rolled out onto the main line. Others, brandishing pistols and cursing the thieving Yankees, ran after the train, now rapidly outdistancing them.

From atop the tender, Fuller watched Murphy sprinting to get aboard. He saw the Irishman jump for a hand and foot hold on the rear platform of the baggage car. Several men grabbed his arms and pulled him on.

Two minutes later Murphy had made his way through the baggage car and across to the tender. His tie was loose and his hair disheveled as he climbed up onto the pile of coal. "Damn it, Fuller, I had the *New York* ready to go!" he exploded. "Why'd you take this one? It's smaller and slower . . . a mogul engine with little drive wheels . . . ," he panted, sweat streaking his red face. "Built for power, not for speed. Besides, the *New York* is owned by our own road."

"This was handier," Fuller replied calmly. Leaving Murphy grumbling that the race was lost, Fuller climbed down into the cab, then eased out onto the narrow, wooden catwalk and around to the pilot beam on the front of the engine.

A mile farther on, he spotted something ahead and yelled for Hardin to stop. Several men piled out of the baggage car to clear about twenty loose cross-ties from the track. Fuller caught Murphy's eye, and pointed at the broken telegraph wire dangling from a nearby pole.

"They're a damned determined bunch," Murphy said.

"Or desperate," Fuller replied.

In a matter of minutes, the way was cleared and everyone scrambled back into the baggage car. There was no shouting or wild excitement now. The mood of the men had become as grim and dark as the overcast, misty weather.

As they got under way again, Fuller carefully shifted his position from side to side on the pilot beam so he'd always be on the insides of curves to watch for obstructions. Murphy was right — the *William R. Smith* was a much slower locomotive. Or else Hardin was unable or unwilling to hazard greater speed because of the wet, slick rails.

The steam whistle wailed its drawn-out, mournful cry for an approaching crossing, and Fuller saw a Negro pull his span of mules to a halt to wait for them to pass.

As the *General* finally cleared the siding at Kingston and began to move, Carrick edged away from the heat of the open fire door and leaned out the left side of the cab to catch the cooling breeze on his face.

They had been stuck here for over an hour. He was glad that Andrews had the aplomb to remain calm and unruffled. But, as soon as the *General*, its tender, and three boxcars were well clear of Kingston, Andrews began showing strain.

"All right, boys, let's push her!" he said. "We have to meet a through freight and a passenger train at Adairsville. That delay has put us behind schedule, but those up ahead should be waiting for us to pass."

Knight and Wilson needed no further orders. The

fireman heaped split logs into the firebox as fast as Carrick could pass them down from the tender. Every time Wilson's gloved hand swung open the cast iron door, Carrick felt the blast of heat from the roaring fire.

But they were hardly up to full speed when Andrews ordered them to stop again. "It's only ten miles to Adairsville, and we could be delayed there, too. To make sure we slow down our pursuers, let's pull up another rail."

The locomotive slowed. Before they came to a complete stop, Carrick and most of the men from the boxcars were on the ground. About half the raiders were gathering brush and spare ties along the right-of-way to use in burning upcoming bridges. The rain was increasing and the wood was damp, so Andrews urged them to gather as much fuel as they could. Meanwhile, he sent Scott up the nearest pole to cut the telegraph wire.

"Mother, you've been through enough," Josiah Waymier said as Amelia climbed down. "Why don't you stay in the cab and rest?"

"I can at least gather brush," she said, ignoring his advice.

He shrugged, and went to work on the rails.

Some of the strongest men found that pulling up a rail with only one crowbar for a tool was hard, frustrating work. Several took turns with the bar, slowing prying and pounding out spike after spike from the unforgiving oak ties. When they'd freed about two-thirds of a rail from its fastenings, eight men, including Carrick, gripped the loosened end and tried to use the rail as a lever to pry out the remaining spikes.

"Okay, men, *heave!*" Andrews cried.

The men strained, but nothing gave.

"Again!"

The eight strained, but the spikes remained fast in the wood.

Just then the faint, but unmistakable, wail of a distant locomotive steam whistle sent a shudder through their midst. Fear stabbed at Carrick's innards as he let go of the rail. A shocked expression marked every face as the men turned to look behind them. Carrick thought of the two trains four miles ahead that were possibly blocking the tracks. And now, from the south, came the sound of a pursuing engine, and it would be on them in a couple of minutes.

They didn't need to be told what to do. The eight men crouched and grabbed the free end of the rail once more.

"Ready?" Carrick yelled. *"Now!"*

The men thrust upward with their legs, biceps bulging, corded necks straining as they lifted with every ounce of their combined strength. The rail bent under the terrible pressure of panic, and suddenly snapped with a *twang!* The men tumbled in a confused heap down the graded bank. But they were quickly on their feet and, throwing their piece of rail into a boxcar, jumped aboard. Knight opened the throttle, and they were off, quickly gaining speed.

For the moment they were safe, Carrick thought, as, panting and sweating, he climbed to his place atop the rocking tender. But what disorder from unscheduled trains and delays lay ahead of them at Adairsville?

The *William R. Smith* and its two cars, running in reverse, were still four miles from Adairsville when Fuller, squinting ahead into a fine, driving rain, spotted a break in the left-hand rail.

"Stop! Stop!" He leaned out to the side and frantically waved at the engineer. Alert, Hardin threw off the throttle and applied the brakes. Even though their speed wasn't great, the broken rail seemed to be rushing toward them. The cars would fall to the left. Fuller was looking for a place to jump off the right side, when the wheels spun in reverse, sliding on the wet rails, and finally drew the heavy locomotive to a stop only yards short of the gap. With trembling legs, Fuller climbed down and walked back to the cab. "Looks like a six-foot break in the left rail. Get some of those men to yank up a rail from behind us to replace the missing one."

"Good idea," Hardin said, leaning on the window armrest. "But we don't have a single track tool of any kind aboard."

"I know they'll be stopped at Adairsville," Fuller said. "I'm going ahead on foot."

"The *Texas* should be arriving there, pulling a downward bound freight," Murphy said. "I'm coming with you."

"Jeff, your lungs won't stand all this running, especially in the rain," Fuller said. "Go on back with Hardin and this train and wait for us at Kingston."

Cain nodded his assent.

"Get some men and tools to fix this rail!" Murphy called over his shoulder as he and Fuller jogged away down the track toward Adairsville.

"Damned glad to be away from that wild bunch in the baggage car," Fuller said between breaths as he and Murphy slipped and slid along the muddy right-of-way. "They'd be shootin' everybody in sight if we catch up to those Yanks!"

The running was slow going, and Fuller quit talking to save his breath. The sticky limestone mud was nearly as viscous as tar and it built up on the thick soles of Fuller's boots, making each foot feel like it was carrying a ten-pound weight. Every few minutes he had to stop and scrape off the mud on the rails, taking advantage of the pause to suck more air into his laboring lungs. He wiped his nose with the back of his hand, and it came away smeared with blood. It seemed like hours since he'd started out on foot from Big Shanty. At the rate they were going, he and Murphy would never overtake the *General* before it left Adairsville.

Chapter Ten
a hard decision

Bent over and gasping, hands on knees, and the increasing rain beginning to seep through the seams of his coat, Fuller was near despair. Why was he killing himself like this? Wounded pride that his train had been taken from him by several brazen Yankees? He was determined they would not get away with it. From long experience, he knew most of the road's schedule by heart, and a southbound freight, under command of Conductor Sam Downs, should be along any time now. If he could just get his breath and hold out a little longer.

As Murphy came puffing up with a concerned look, Fuller straightened and nodded that he was OK. Forcing himself into a slipping, staggering run, he and Murphy went on.

After another mile, Fuller saw smoke belching above the trees. It was moving slowly toward them. He signaled Murphy to stop, and he stood, sucking in great lungs full of cool, damp air as he watched the train approach.

"It's the *Texas*, just as I figured!" Fuller cried, running and waving both arms. He recognized Pete Bracken at the controls, and the engineer threw on the brakes. The heavy locomotive was slowing its long freight of twenty-one cars as it passed the two men and rolled another thirty yards before Bracken could halt his momentum in a hissing cloud of steam and screeching iron wheels.

Fuller jogged to the footplate of the locomotive. "Sam! Some Yankee raiders stole the *General.*"

"What? Then they sure made a fool of me with that tale about running a special powder train to General Beauregard." He gave a disgusted shake of his head. "Talked me right out of their way."

Fuller pulled himself up onto the lower step of the cab. "Sam, back 'er into Adairsville and we'll drop all these cars. Then, we'll give 'em a run for it."

"Nothing I'd like better!"

Fuller joined the engineer and fireman in the cab as Murphy climbed up the side of the tender.

Bracken threw the chest-high lever into reverse, and opened the throttle. Fuller glanced at the steam gauge and noted with satisfaction that the *Texas* was at full pressure. Both the *Texas* and the *General* were 4-4-0, American-type locomotives, very similar in size and power, but the *Texas* was handicapped just now with the weight of a seven-hundred-foot-long string of loaded freight cars as it chugged slowly back toward Adairsville.

Bracken coaxed all the power he could from the engine and shoved the train, full steam, for two miles to the depot. As they approached Adairsville and began to slow, Fuller jumped off and ran ahead, throwing the switch to the siding so the caboose could run off, followed by the string of freight cars. When they had all passed him and stopped, Fuller slipped in behind the tender and pulled the coupling pin. Stepping out, he waved for Bracken to pull forward, then closed the switch to the siding.

Fuller mounted the cab and looked at the bearded Sam

Bracken. "How fast can you make it to Calhoun?" he asked.

"Check your watch," Bracken replied, grimly. "It's ten miles. For every minute over ten, I'll give you a dollar."

Fuller's pounding heart and nerves were so frayed when they reached Calhoun that he never looked at his watch.

"Ten minutes flat!" Bracken said, pulling his watch from the pocket of his overalls as he eased the engine down to eight miles an hour.

Ahead, two miles north of Calhoun, Andrews ordered Knight to stop the *General* in a low swag in the terrain where they couldn't readily be seen.

"Get another rail up, and be quick about it!" he yelled, springing down from the cab.

Amelia Waymier, scrambling out of the way of the four men in the cab, climbed to sit with Gibson Carrick on the stacked wood atop the tender.

"Here we go again," Carrick said, grinning at her as he slid down the iron ladder to join the other raiders spilling out of the boxcars. But removing a rail here was no easier than before. Lacking the proper tools, they began the laborious task of battering and prying up several spikes from the stubborn wood at one end of a rail.

Grunting and sweating, the men worked silently. They managed to free several spikes from the south end of the rail. Then, thinking to hurry the rest of the job, one man wedged a long sapling under the rail and pried up. But the green wood bent like a bow while the rail hardly moved. He swore under his breath in frustration. "Can't get any leverage with this!"

"Grab a couple of those fence rails!" Sergeant-Major Ross yelled.

Three men kicked down a nearby rail fence bordering a

cornfield. The stiffer poles gave more power, but, just as the men lifted and the rail began to bend slightly, the wail of a steam whistle came loud and clear from the south!

Carrick's heart skipped a beat, and he felt the blood draining from his flushed face. The men stopped as one, staring, open-mouthed.

Another shrill, wavering howl sounded, even closer this time.

"Let's go! Get aboard!" Andrews shouted as the locomotive, running in reverse and trailing smoke, came into view about a half mile behind them.

Carrick and Andrews, with the aid of Josiah Waymier and one other man, wedged two fence posts under the slightly bent rail.

"There!" Andrews panted, brushing his hands on his trousers. "That'll keep the end of the rail up a few inches. Even if it doesn't derail 'em, they'll have to stop and straighten it."

But, for the first time, Carrick saw doubt on the face of their leader.

"Everyone into the forward boxcars!" Andrews cried, waving them ahead. "Carrick, pull the pin between those cars. We've got to do something to slow 'em down." Andrews bit at his lower lip as Carrick sprang to obey.

After leaving Adairsville, the men had used ties as battering rams to break openings in the ends of each boxcar. This allowed easy passage between cars and provided some additional, splintered firewood for the engine.

Even as he worked at the coupling, Carrick was surprised at the order. A boxcar left on the track would not slow down the pursuing engine. But it *would* mean the loss of a car full of cross-ties, fence posts, and brush the raiders had gathered at random for use as fuel to burn bridges. Was

Andrews becoming desperate?

"Pour some oil inside and fire it," Andrews said when the pin was pulled.

Knight handed down the long-spouted oilcan to Carrick who squirted several jets of oil into the splintered opening, soaking a tangled pile of vines and brush. Then he struck a match to it in several places. The oil caught, but the flames spread slowly upward through the wet brush. The flames were reaching for the heavier wood, but Carrick suspected the oil would burn off without catching much else afire. On a dry day with the wind blowing, the whole fuel-laden car would have been engulfed within minutes.

"Now, give 'er a good shove!" Andrews ordered.

Knight reversed the engine. Several short jets of smoke chuffed from the stack as the *General* accelerated. Carrick and Andrews stood to one side and watched the train pick up speed. Then Knight hit the brakes and pulled the engine to a stop. The uncoupled boxcar gently coasted away, trailing smoke from its open doors. But the grade was very slight and Carrick knew the flaming car posed little hazard to their pursuers.

Knight brought the *General* chugging back the quarter mile and slowed to pick up Andrews and Carrick.

"Let's stop and fight 'em, Mister Andrews!" one of the men yelled from the open door of the boxcar. "They couldn't have many men on that engine. We can whip 'em!"

Another man waved a pistol out the broken opening in the forward end of the car. "We're tired of running like scared rabbits!"

Three or four others chimed in their assent.

"That's not our purpose," Andrews replied, swinging aboard the slowly rolling locomotive. Carrick grabbed the ladder of the tender.

"The Oostanaula River bridge is coming up pretty soon, Mister Andrews," young Waymier said from his seat on the left side of the cab.

As the *General* gained speed, Andrews didn't reply. He looked back, and then forward toward the long, seventy-five yard approach to the wooden trestle.

"You going to set it afire?" Amelia Waymier asked as the bridge grew larger ahead of them.

"Can't," Andrews replied grimly, looking back at the pursuing locomotive that had fallen about two miles to their rear. It had been forced to stop and flatten the raised rail and then to catch the rolling boxcar.

From this distance Carrick saw no evidence of smoke from the yellow, wooden car. He guessed the fire had probably gone out of its own accord.

"No time to stop," Andrews continued. "They're pressing us too close."

From atop the diminished woodpile on the tender, Carrick heard these words with a sinking feeling in the pit of his stomach. It wasn't just Andrews's words, but their tone. Andrews had so far been their center of calm in this whirlwind raid. But now he was showing signs of doubt. He didn't want to stand and fight — a wise decision, Carrick thought, since they didn't know the strength of the Rebels, and it would only delay them further in case any others were chasing. Then there was Amelia Waymier to think of. . . . It seemed all their best-laid plans were going awry. Somehow, in spite of the obstructions they'd rigged, a locomotive was only minutes behind them. It was demoralizing. They couldn't possibly fire this bridge — one of their main objectives. It would probably take at least an hour to get a blaze going in the misty rain, even if they could find enough dry combustibles — a doubtful prospect. But now it was not a matter of having leisure to stop and kindle a big fire; it was a matter of hot pursuit with a Confederate locomotive in view.

Andrews looked regretfully at the crucial bridge as they rolled up onto the wooden structure. Carrick could almost read his thoughts. If they could somehow destroy this bridge, or make it impassable, they would be safe, as would the whole of East Tennessee. But if wishes were gold bars. . . .

"Gold bars!" Carrick almost shouted. "Mister Andrews! Could we outrun them if we weren't carrying all those gold and silver bars?"

"I'd forgotten all about them. Stop on the bridge! We'll jettison that load."

The *General*'s brakes squealed as it halted halfway across the trestle.

"You'll *what?*" Amelia scrambled down off the tender into the cab and confronted Andrews.

"We'll get rid of all that weight. Then maybe we'll have a chance to outrun them," Andrews said.

"Over my dead body!" Amelia snapped, looking up at the big man. He gave ground instinctively at this sudden outburst until he was against the side of the cab. "Not after all the trouble and pain I went through to get that treasure for the Yankees and myself!" she cried. "I gave up my home and everything I had. A couple thousand extra pounds isn't going to make any difference to a steam locomotive."

"It just might make the difference between living and dying," Andrews retorted, regaining his composure.

"Ridiculous!" Amelia snapped, as if she were admonishing a naughty child. "If we can't escape *with* that gold, then we certainly can't get away without it, either. It's not heavy enough to make a difference."

"Hurrah for Missus Waymier!" A cheer rose from the men who'd crowded the open ends of the boxcars and climbed the back of the tender to see why they'd stopped. Josiah's fair complexion began to redden, and he slid out of his seat, as if looking for a place to hide.

"Look, Missus Waymier," Andrews said, holding up his hand to silence the rowdy men behind him, "if the Rebs catch us, they'll get the bullion right back. Do you want that?"

Several seconds of tension filled the tiny cab. The softly panting locomotive could be clearly heard in the sudden silence.

"Well . . . ?" Andrews finally asked. "Better make up your mind, and be quick about it."

"Let's put it to a vote," Alf Wilson said, wiping his sweating brow with the back of his heavy glove.

"No vote!" Andrews snapped instantly. "We'll decide this between us."

"Then let each man take a bar and pitch the rest into the river," Amelia said with a sigh, "before they get close enough to see what we're doing."

"Agreed." Andrews gave the order to the listening men. Willing hands began to pound the lids off the crates.

"One each!" Andrews yelled at them. "Then heave the rest out the door into the water. Move! We haven't got much time! Take the gold, dump the silver."

In a matter of seconds, the boxes began to tumble out the side doors, turning in the air, splashing into the water like a series of huge cannon balls. For the next several minutes, the muddy river churned with the expensive bombardment.

"The Rebs might be able to retrieve that from the bottom," Andrews said, watching, "but it'll be a mighty tough job. The weight'll take it down into the soft mud."

Carrick reached over the back of the tender to heave up one bar at a time and pass them along to the men in the engine.

"You might have to use this to club a Reb," Andrews grumped as he handed the gleaming yellow metal to Amelia. She took the heavy bar in both hands and set it down beside her.

"I think she deserves at least two of those," Carrick said.

Andrews glanced sharply at him. "She'll play hell toting even one if we have to abandon this train and take to our heels," he said. "But I suppose you're right," he continued in a softer tone. "Pass up another bar." He had to raise his voice to make himself heard above the men who were arguing. "What's the trouble there?"

"There ain't quite enough gold ones to go around!" one of the men yelled back. "Just a few mixed gold and silver bars left. . . ."

"Then give me a gold one up here!" Andrews ordered, climbing up past Carrick. "I don't think you have to worry about spending it anyway," he muttered, barely loud enough for Carrick's ears.

It was the second time Andrews had revealed his doubts. Carrick looked for the pursuing train, but saw only puffing smoke rising above a patch of woods about a mile behind. At least, the trees would screen them from view while they dumped the bullion. Maybe the Rebs would never know to look in the river. If the pursuers noticed them stopped on the bridge, they'd likely assume it was for the purpose of setting it afire.

"All done!" Sergeant-Major Ross called.

Andrews nodded curtly. "Let's fire another boxcar, leave it, and then move!"

Once the second boxcar was detached, Knight eased open the throttle. Carrick could hear the trestle creak under their weight as the wheels began to turn.

"Wilson, get to stoking!" Andrews snapped. Alf Wilson was startled from running his hands over the yellow bar of gold on the footplate beside him. He pulled on his gloves and went to work.

Carrick passed down the wood, noting how low the pile was getting. They would have to stop and wood up before long.

They rolled off the end of the bridge and began to pick up speed as they passed through the tiny village of Resaca. Andrews resumed his place beside Josiah Waymier who was in the left-hand seat where his normally clear view was blurred as heavy rain streaked the glass. In order to see ahead, he thrust his head out, shielding his eyes with his hat brim.

His mother had rejoined Carrick and was helping to pass wood from the back of the tender.

"We climb a gradual grade away from the river for a few miles," Josiah said. "Need to keep up steam."

"You heard him," Andrews said to Wilson who was already busy feeding the voracious firebox.

"They're slowing down at the bridge," Carrick said, standing up with his feet braced for a better view over the remaining boxcar.

Andrews leaned far out the left side of the cab for a look. "Probably want to make sure we didn't damage it. I'm certain they didn't see us throw those crates overboard."

"Green's wood yard two miles ahead," Josiah said.

"What about it, Wilson?"

"We've *got* to wood up," the fireman answered, never pausing in his rhythmic, swinging motion. Half bent at the waist, he heaved in a log and clanged the fire door shut, then pivoted to receive another length of cordwood. Swinging back, he kicked open the iron door, and repeated the process.

As the *General* labored up out of the river valley, the timber around them grew thicker and they temporarily lost sight of the locomotive behind. Knight kept up all the speed he could until they were almost to the wood yard, then he slammed on the brakes and reversed the big drive wheels, skidding to a halt.

The superintendent of the wood yard seemed intimidated by the sight of the twenty bearded men swarming off the shattered boxcar and helping themselves to the neatly stacked cordwood. He looked on, wide-eyed, without even requesting the ticket from Knight.

Andrews and Amelia worked on the ground with the rest, frantically passing split wood. As the *General* hissed and panted softly, short logs of hardwood clattered and banged into the tender.

"Special powder train for General Beauregard!" Andrews yelled over his shoulder at the startled Green. The cover story had lost all plausibility, Carrick thought. But it hardly mattered, as the wood tender didn't even act as if he'd heard.

Carrick paused once for breath and saw Andrews staring south for sign of the pursuers.

"We can capture that train if you're willing," Carrick said.

"How?"

"Find a good place on a curve where there are plenty of bushes, put some obstruction on the track, and hide. Knight can run the *General* on ahead out of sight. When the Rebs stop to clear the track, we'll rush 'em. After we capture them, Knight can reverse their engine and send it back down the track at full speed, either to wreck or stop anyone else who might be following."

"It's a good plan," Andrews said thoughtfully. "Might be worth a try."

The wail of a distant steam whistle yanked all heads in a southerly direction.

Chapter Eleven
Burning

"Damned determined devils," Andrews muttered. "Keep loading, men. We still have a few more minutes," he added calmly.

The line of wood passers resumed.

The insistent shrieking of the whistle seemed to be screaming a warning at the wood yard supervisor, but Green was still standing as if in a stupor, staring at the frantic activity of the men who were depleting his fuel supply.

"All right, that's enough," Andrews finally said as the whistle screeched just out of sight around the bend.

The men leaped for the train. Alf Wilson was the last to board, lugging one more huge armload of wood. Even so, they had managed to load only about three-fourths of a cord, Carrick estimated, running his eye over the pile of split oak.

"There's a water tower at Tilton, about three miles ahead," Josiah said as the *General* lurched into motion.

"We have to slow 'em down some more," Andrews said. "Pass the word to pitch out a few more of those cross-ties!" he shouted up to Carrick, who then relayed the order. Several seconds later he saw the ties tumbling out the back of the broken boxcar. Most of them showed an irritating tendency to bounce end over end off the tracks. Only a few came to rest across one or both rails.

Amelia stayed in the cab, but kept back out of the way of Knight and Wilson. Every minute or so, Wilson aimed the long snout of the oilcan at the open fire door and gave the blaze a few squirts to make it burn even hotter.

Carrick saw the tiny village of Tilton coming up, and Knight held his speed until the last possible second before he applied the brakes. But the *General* skidded to a stop a few yards beyond the water tower. Knight cursed himself softly as he threw the engine into reverse and backed into position.

Before they were even stopped, Wilson was out of the cab. He climbed to the top of the locomotive, grabbed the overhead pipe, and swung it down.

"Those cross-ties must have delayed 'em some," Knight said.

Andrews nodded. "Yeah, we've got a little breathing room for now."

"Full!" Wilson yelled, flinging the still-gushing spout away from the engine. He scrambled back down along the catwalk into the cab as the engineer opened the throttle. Wheels spun briefly, and they were off once more.

"Fairly straight and level to Dalton," Josiah told them.

"Pour on the steam!" came Andrews's terse voice.

Knight opened the throttle, and the *General* surged ahead faster and faster.

From his perch on the tender, Carrick could see the men in the boxcar just behind being flung about like kernels of popcorn in a hot pan. Without the steadying influence of several more cars, the boxcar felt every jerk and motion of the powerful engine. It was being yanked from side to side like the end of a whip.

Carrick had to lie down just to keep his balance as he shoved the firewood forward to Wilson. Carrick thought he'd seen the *General*'s top speed before, but now they seemed to be flying. The only thing keeping them from careening off into a pile of scalding wreckage was the tenuous grip of the wheel flanges on the insides of the thin strips of metal. The top-heavy engine rocked violently from side to side, as if trying to break the friction of the iron rails. From his face-down position, he saw a continuous stream of sparks pouring back on either side of the big drivers.

Bushes and trees became a green blur, and Carrick, to avoid dizziness, focused to the front. The wet, shining rails stretched ahead until they appeared to meet in the distance. Then, even that vision blurred as wood smoke was flattened from the balloon stack and whipped back over the tender, stinging tears from his eyes.

Aboard the *Texas*, engineer Bracken pulled the looped, overhead cord, releasing a long, wailing burst from the steam whistle, followed by two shorter ones as he flicked his wrist with practiced ease. "By God, look at 'em scramble!" Bracken yelled as the *General* and its boxcars came in sight a little over a mile ahead. He yanked the whistle cord again.

Fuller could barely make out some tiny figures mounting the *General* as it began to gather speed. In less than a minute, their quarry had steamed beyond their vision into a patch of woods, the smoke blending with the gray overcast sky.

"How many men you reckon they got?" Bracken asked.

"Not more than four . . . five at the most," Fuller replied thoughtfully.

"Well, we got six, and two of 'em have shotguns besides

their pistols," Bracken said confidently. "I joined this chase late, but you're right to keep crowdin' them. If we come up with that bunch, there'll be a fight for sure. Yankees or not, anybody who has the brass to sneak into enemy territory and snatch a train like they done ain't gonna give up without a scrap."

"It wouldn't be bravery," Fuller replied, his eyes still scanning the tracks for obstructions. "If men are too cowardly to wear the uniform when they fight, I haven't got much use for 'em. No . . . if we catch 'em, they'll only fight like cornered animals . . . to save their hides."

"Still, I think it might be wise to hold up and wait for a train with reinforcements," Murphy said.

Fuller could feel the heat rising in his neck and face. He took off his hat to wipe a bandanna across his baldpate. "Not on your life. That was *my* train they took, and I'll get it back or die trying."

Because the *Texas* was still steaming in reverse, Fuller, Murphy, and the two men with shotguns were perched at the rear of the tender, keeping a look-out

"Brake!" one of the look-outs yelled.

Bracken instantly slammed the brake lever, and the engine quickly slowed.

Fuller swung out and dropped to the ground while they were still rolling. One end of a rail had been pried up a few inches and a fence post wedged underneath. Fuller and Murphy pulled it out, and signaled for the engine to come ahead slowly. The wheels flattened the rail into position, and they rolled over it safely. The two men swung aboard, and the engine picked up speed. But Fuller was nervous. "I've got to get up where I can see." He climbed the ladder into the tender, and crawled back to the brake wheel.

Two miles farther ahead he spotted a lone boxcar. It appeared to be rolling slowly toward them, trailing a little smoke.

"Slow! Slow!" He waved a warning at Bracken. "Careful. She's smoking. Could be a bomb in that car." His stomach was tense as he ordered the two men with the shotguns to clear the train, just in case. Risking his own life was one thing, but putting volunteers in jeopardy was quite another.

The *Texas* came to a standstill, then Bracken eased the engine forward, allowing the rolling thirty-two-foot yellow boxcar gently to bump the back of the tender.

Fuller, holding his breath, thrust his head through the hole in the end of the car and let out a sigh of relief. "No bomb!" he called over his shoulder. "Just a lot of brush and cross-ties and hunks of wood. Looks like they tried to set it afire, but only some of it burned."

Fuller waved the two volunteers back aboard while he climbed to the top of the boxcar and sat straddling the rear brake wheel where he had a good view of the track ahead. He signaled Bracken to reverse the *Texas* again. He realized they had to keep pressing and scanned the rails ahead for obstructions. The car full of wood and brush told him the raiders might try to burn the Oostanaula River bridge, or one of the smaller ones over Chicamauga Creek near Ringgold.

A short time later they sped around a long left-hand curve and saw the Oostanaula bridge at Resaca, still intact a half mile ahead. Fuller's stomach tensed as he spotted the *General*, its tender and one boxcar fleeing off the far end of the partially covered bridge.

"Take it easy!" he called back to Bracken. "They've dropped another car."

Bracken slowed, and came cautiously toward the approach. Pushing the tender and boxcar in reverse, they crept up into the dim tunnel of the semi-covered bridge. Sections of wood several feet wide alternated with gaps the same width on the walls of the covered bridge.

"This car's on fire, too!" Fuller yelled back. "Come ahead slow and pick it up."

The smoldering boxcar trailed white smoke from its shattered end as they shoved it off the undamaged bridge. The raiders hadn't gained enough time to fire the wet bridge, Fuller thought, not even to throw a scoop or two of hot coals from the firebox.

Fuller stopped at the siding switch just beyond the river at Resaca and shunted off the two boxcars, leaving the *Texas* and its tender free. But he realized that dropping the two boxcars had delayed them just enough to allow the *General* to reach Green's wood yard and replenish their fuel. He gritted his teeth in grim determination. The raiders weren't being allowed enough time to stop and destroy any bridges. In fact, they were becoming so desperate they were dropping their boxcars full of combustible fuel that they might have used on one of the several small bridges over Chicamauga Creek. Destroying any one of these bridges, however small, would effectively cut off pursuit by rail.

At his look-out post on the rear of the tender, Fuller pulled a small notebook and pencil from his coat pocket. Keeping an eye on the rails ahead, he braced himself against the train's motion and managed to scribble a telegraphic message:

> To General Ledbetter, Cmdr. at Chattanooga
>
> My train was captured this a.m. at Big Shanty, evidently by Federal soldiers in disguise. They are making rapidly for Chattanooga, possibly with the

idea of burning the railroad bridges in their rear. If I do not capture them in the meantime, see that they do not pass Chattanooga.

Conductor William Fuller

Just as he was tucking the notebook into his pocket, he spotted two cross-ties on the rails. "Stop! Stop!" he shouted a warning to Bracken.

Fuller had attached a long bar to the brake wheel of the tender to give leverage in helping the engine make fast stops, and now he shoved hard against it, feeling the brakes take hold.

"Damn!" Bracken slammed the chest-high Johnson bar into another quadrant, activating the reverse valve rod. This allowed steam to enter the cylinders out of sequence, spinning the wheels in reverse.

Fuller hung on, knowing this hazardous procedure, if done too quickly or at high speed, could blow out a cylinder head, and the resulting flat spots on the iron driving wheels were an added irritation to any good engineer. Once again, the *Texas* skidded to a halt, and the men jumped down to clear the track.

The Yankees had done their work well. Three times within the next mile the *Texas* stopped for similar obstructions.

As they approached the wood yard, Bracken frantically blasted the steam whistle. *Maybe Green will be alerted that something is wrong before he supplies the raiders with wood,* Fuller thought.

Bracken slowed the *Texas* near the wood yard.

"When did they leave?" Fuller shouted from his perch atop the tender.

"Just a few minutes ago!" came the reply.

Bracken threw the throttle open, and they began to move.

They'd gone less than a quarter mile before Fuller spotted two more cross-ties on the rails. With frustrating interruptions, the chase continued.

Two miles below Dalton, they approached the water tank at the hamlet of Tilton. The spout had very recently been left down, and the men on the tender and in the cab could not avoid a good dousing from the gushing spout as they passed underneath.

"Another reason I want to get my hands on them," Fuller muttered, wiping the water from his face.

"We're ahead of the regular schedule," Andrews said as they came in sight of Dalton, the largest town since Marietta. "Stop so I can check the switch."

The *General* stopped some distance below the big depot. Andrews ran forward to be sure the switch was in the proper position to carry them along the main line to Chattanooga, instead of shunting them off in the direction of Cleveland and Knoxville.

Carrick saw him say something to three railroad workers in overalls, but couldn't hear the words. Andrews was back in the cab within two minutes. "Blast right through here," he instructed Knight.

The engineer opened the throttle. By the time they reached the depot, the train was traveling at least forty-five. A passenger shed extended out over both tracks and the *General* roared under it, smoke billowing and obscuring the startled faces of the passengers waiting on the platform.

"Slow down!" Josiah cried, gripping the armrest in the window. "Mill Creek Gap coming up. Sharp left-hand curve!"

Too late, Knight threw off the power as the top-heavy engine careened into the curve. Carrick hurled himself flat on the woodpile and grabbed for the left side of the tender, sensing the wheels lift from the inside rail. He held his breath as the *General* leaned far to the right. Carrick thought they were goners. A tortured *squeal* of metal against metal cut through the noise while the locomotive struggled to right itself. For the space of four heartbeats, the *General* balanced on the edge of disaster. Then it rocked back onto its wheels and began to slow. They had somehow defied the pull of inertia, Carrick thought, looking up, his mouth and throat dry. Knight slumped into the right-hand seat and let the engine roll almost a mile as their speed decreased.

"This is as good a place as any to stop and cut that wire before they can send a message from Dalton," Andrews said.

Two men boosted Scott up the nearest pole, and he used the short saw to rip through the wire.

"The line just went dead," the young telegraph operator at the Dalton depot said to Fuller.

"How much got through?"

"All but the last sentence and your name."

Fuller nodded with satisfaction. "You did a quick job without asking any questions. That may just be what we needed to head them off."

He sprinted out the door for the train. The *Texas* was rolling as he swung aboard.

Chapter Twelve
man against machine

"Mister Andrews, are we going to ambush them in the tunnel?" Sergeant-Major Marion Ross asked as the raiders scrambled back into the boxcar from piling another dozen ties on the tracks.

Atop the tender, Carrick caught the words and paused to watch the exchange of the two men standing just below him.

"They're pressing us too closely," Andrews replied. "No time."

"I could do it," Ross said in a self-assured tone.

"No, no." Andrews shook his head. "Get aboard."

"One man, one cross-tie. That's all it would take."

"And kill yourself? No. Besides, they'll come in there cautiously and see the tie on the tracks just like they did before. They'll stop and remove it. Won't delay 'em but a couple o' minutes, and you'd be captured besides."

"Let me try," Ross urged. "It's too good a chance to waste. These soggy bridges won't burn."

For the first time, Andrews seemed to take him seriously. He turned and looked the stocky Ross squarely in the eye. "Do you know what you're proposing? If you succeed in derailing that train in the tunnel, you'll be killed. If you don't succeed, you'll be captured or shot."

"Somebody's got to do it, Mister Andrews. I don't have a family. And I'm big and strong enough to wrestle one of these cross-ties into position."

Without giving Andrews a chance to object, he dashed back to the open door of the boxcar and began dragging out a big cross-tie.

Andrews hesitated but didn't try to stop him. Carrick was the only witness to this drama as everyone else was preparing to get under way. Knight craned his neck back to see if Andrews had given the signal, but the big, bearded leader was now saying something to Ross out of Carrick's hearing. Andrews gripped Ross's hand, turned away quickly, grabbed the ladder on the side of the boxcar, and swung up, motioning with his other hand to the engineer. The wheels spun, then caught, and the *General* started rolling.

A mile from Dalton, Fuller spotted the downed line, and the now familiar cross-ties piled on the tracks. In the three minutes it took them to clear the obstacle, he also noticed a few wooden levers where the raiders had abandoned another attempt to pry up a rail.

Fuller climbed back to the cab of the *Texas*, and they got under way. There were no more ties on the tracks, and Bracken gradually increased their speed.

Just over three miles later, Andrews ordered Knight to stop the *General* outside the mouth of the tunnel. Ross jumped down, dragging the tie with him. Much to the surprise of the other men, Knight immediately started up again, and they rolled into the blackness of the tunnel, accelerating quickly. Smoke blotted everything and Carrick tucked his nose and mouth into the crook of his arm, shutting his eyes against the acrid, choking cloud that was deflected down onto them from the low ceiling. He held his breath as they steamed through the long tunnel, the deafening racket of the pounding locomotive being thrown back from the stone walls on either side. Finally he could focus on the bright opening at the far end that was rapidly getting larger as they rushed toward it, but his thoughts were on the man they'd left behind. He was certain he'd looked his last on Sergeant-Major Marion Ross — a man who was giving himself for the success of their mission.

As Ross watched the splintered end of the boxcar disappear into the tunnel, he had a sudden qualm of fear. He was on his own now; his friends were gone. Had he been too hasty in volunteering for this suicide mission? Was he really ready to die? He thrust the doubt aside. He was as likely to be killed leading men into battle as he was here, and for less reason. In any case, his job as a sergeant-major was to set an example for the men.

The chuffing roar and *clatter* of the *General* receded into the blackness, leaving only the gray veil of wood smoke drifting out of the stone archway. The feeling of sudden isolation was only fleeting; he had work to do. He stooped, wrapped his arms around the squared-off log, and lifted. The cross-tie was taller than his head — and heavy. As he struggled awkwardly to drag it into the tunnel, he heard the distant wail of a steam whistle. He felt a surge of adrenaline. He had to hurry. He cast a quick glance back, but the locomotive was still out of sight beyond a row of trees bordering a small stream.

Ignoring the scrapes on his hands and wrists from the rough wood, he locked his right arm around one end of the tie and pulled, dragging it as fast as he could move into the dimness. The heavy timber bumped across the ties between the rails, threatening to jerk itself out of his grip. He had to get far enough inside where they wouldn't see the obstruction until it was too late. Their temporary blindness as they came suddenly out of the light would help his cause.

"Tunnel Hill coming up soon," Fuller said, after three more miles had passed under their wheels.

Bracken gave a pull on the overhead cord, and the steam whistle responded with a long, screeching wail.

"Perfect place for an ambush," Murphy replied. The strain of the chase had not seemed to wear down the big Irishman. His tie was gone and his white shirt smudged with mud and soot, but he still looked eager for the chase.

"Wouldn't have to be an ambush with guns," Bracken said. "They could put something on the tracks that would derail us."

"That'd jam the tunnel and block the line as good as burning a bridge," Murphy commented.

"Or they could run the *General*, full-speed, right back at us," Bracken continued, looking at Fuller who was trying to visualize the consequences of such an action. "The boilers would likely explode on impact," Bracken added. "If we aren't all sent to perdition by the crash, we'll be flayed alive by the steam."

"How long is that tunnel?" Murphy asked. "Maybe we could see daylight at the other end and know if it was blocked."

"Nearly five hundred yards," Bracken said. "Even smoke could block the tiny bit of light at the other end until we're well inside."

The *Texas*, pushing its tender, was traveling fifty miles an hour in reverse, the wind trailing the smoke from the stack away behind them. In the few seconds while each man considered the possibilities, the only sounds to be heard were the chuffing and grinding and a cacophony of metallic noises as the machine sped along, each stroke of the pistons carrying them inevitably toward the black void.

Ross now realized he should have had Andrews drop him somewhere inside the tunnel. He was panting with effort and excitement as the whistle sounded again behind him. The Rebs were letting the raiders know they were close. He struggled along — twenty feet, thirty feet, fifty feet. Shifting his slipping grip on the heavy tie, he cursed softly as splinters lanced his callused hands. His breath was coming in gasps now and sweat stung his eyes. He would try to get close to the halfway point — maybe two hundred yards in where the darkness was complete — no possibility of light from either end. The headlamp of the locomotive would not be bright enough to see much of anything in that Stygian atmosphere filled with smoke.

The fireman threw two hunks of wood into the softly roaring blaze. *Clang!* The slamming of the firebox door brought Fuller and Murphy out of their reverie.

"There's Tunnel Hill up ahead," Bracken said, leaning out the side window to see around the tender. "It's your call," he continued, backing off the throttle. The locomotive immediately responded, and they began to lose speed. "Do we slow down and creep in there, or go through hell-bent?" His eyes were bright as he regarded Fuller and Murphy.

The *Texas* slowed to about twenty miles an hour. The grinding brakes dragged the powerful engine down to walking speed. They rolled over a short wooden bridge spanning a tiny branch. As they cleared the trees flanking the stream, Tunnel Hill came into full view a quarter mile ahead, the rails leading through an earthen cut reinforced by rock retaining walls on either side.

Bracken gave a blast on the steam whistle.

Ross heard the wail of the steam whistle. It did not seem to be any closer. If they were careful and crept through the tunnel, they would see the obstruction in time to stop. His plan would be thwarted. He dropped the tie and paused to catch his breath. Wiping a sleeve across his brow, he became aware of the cool dampness. Water dripped on his head from the arched brick ceiling, ground water percolating through the limestone ledges and earth above.

The rough tie lay between the rails, and he sat down on it, facing the way he had come, arms dangling over his knees. Besides the dripping water, he could hear his own breathing in the solitude. Beyond the distant tunnel opening, he could see a slight movement, but it didn't appear to be an engine. He heard nothing. He tried squinting, but it didn't help his focus. Moving to the side of the tunnel to get a slightly better angle of vision, he saw a rail car slowly advancing toward the mouth of the tunnel. It looked to be the black tender of a locomotive, and smoke was billowing up behind it. He felt a sudden rush of elation. For the first time, he realized the engine was running in reverse, pushing its tender. They might have a man or two on the back of the tender, watching the tracks, but they would not have the benefit of the big headlamp on the front of the engine.

His elation was offset by the fact that they had almost come to a stop. Obviously they were not going to come barreling blindly through the tunnel. Andrews had been right;

they would proceed cautiously and watch for an ambush, traps, or missing pieces of rail. Damn!

He extended his arm to lean against the wall — and lost his balance when his fingers encountered nothing. Stumbling to catch himself, he fell into a gap in the stone and fetched up hard against the back of a shallow alcove. A few seconds of exploration gave him the outline of a bricked archway about six feet high, similar to a niche for a statue, but barely two feet deep. Was this a bricked-up doorway? Maybe it was a place for track crews to store tools, or to hang a lantern when working. Then he realized its obvious purpose — an emergency escape, a duck out for anyone caught in the narrow confines of the tunnel when a train was coming.

Once more he moved back and sat down on the cross-tie. The train was hardly moving. But even if they backed cautiously through the tunnel, they couldn't see the tie on the tracks. Or could they? He turned around and looked toward the other end of the tunnel, more than three hundred yards away. His stomach fell. After all his trouble dragging this heavy wood so far, he now realized his mistake. Although light from the opening at the far end appeared as a small, round spot, it was enough to make the rails look like two bands of silver. The trainmen on the approaching tender would have no trouble spotting anything on the track.

He had a sudden urge to just slide into the alcove and let the train pass unmolested, then try to reach Union lines on his own. No. He had come here with the intention of wrecking or delaying the train long enough for his friends to get away. But how? With the rails visible, he would have to drop the cross-tie under their wheels at the last second. Then, he might succeed. He cringed at the thought of the heavy rail car jumping the tracks and smashing him against the stone wall like a bug, but he'd already determined to give up his life if he had to. He'd do what had to be done, and damn the consequences.

Fuller took hold of a grab bar and leaned out the side of the cab to see around the tender. Was it his imagination, or could he detect some gray smoke drifting out of the tunnel mouth four hundred yards ahead? The *General* had either just passed through or the raiders were waiting for them somewhere inside, either with drawn guns, piled cross-ties, or a full head of steam to send the stolen train charging back into them in the dark. The shining rails looked like two tines of a silver fork, feeding them into that gaping mouth to be devoured.

He pulled his head back inside the cab and looked his indecision at Murphy. Their eyes locked for a second or two, then the big Irishman shrugged. "We haven't been cautious all day. Why start now?"

Fuller took a deep breath. "Full throttle," he said to the engineer. "If we leave this world in the next minute, let's go out in a blaze of glory!"

Ross forced himself to concentrate. Time was short. He squatted, and heaved up one end of the tie, standing it on end between the rails. From behind him, he heard the *whoofing* locomotive as it accelerated. He started to lift the big tie. But it was wet from lying on the roadbed and his hands slipped, spiking his palms with several more splinters. Ignoring the pain, he set the beam down and adjusted his grip. As he heaved the tie off to one side, he was startled by the sudden thunder of the train entering the tunnel, two hundred yards from where he stood. It was going full speed!

He struggled back next to the stone wall, holding the tie upright against him and feeling for the duck out. He would blend in with the smoke-blackened tunnel wall until the last possible moment.

He couldn't see the train coming, but the noise was deafening in the confined space — the *clanking, banging,* and *screeching* of wheels. Great clouds of wood smoke blasted from the stack beneath the fourteen-foot, arched ceiling, filling the tunnel. Ross could only sense the tons of bulk rushing toward him in the blackness. His stomach knotted as he held his breath and waited, balancing the tie on its end, poised to let it fall.

The roar was deafening. He felt the rush of cool air being pushed ahead of the speeding train. It was almost on him. Ready. . . . Ready. . . . Now! He shoved the tie.

But he was a split second too late. The wooden beam was still falling when the tender struck it, hurling it aside against the stone wall. It ricocheted, striking Ross a glancing blow on the head, knocking him back into the duck out. The blow stunned him, and he barely felt the concussion of the locomotive hurtling past, three feet away.

His knees buckled, and he slid down the brick archway, falling forward by the rails. The ground seemed to tilt crazily. As his cheek lay against the cool, wet ballast, thick smoke filled his eyes and nose. He coughed and fought for air. Then his reeling senses began to steady, and he struggled up onto his elbows.

The roar suddenly diminished when the train shot out the far end of the tunnel, still in full pursuit. Along with the smoke, he tasted bitter defeat. He struggled to a sitting position and disgustedly watched the train recede. They had decided to blast through under a full head of steam and take their chances. He'd mis-timed his trap by a fraction of a second and failed even to slow it down. It was doubtful the look-out on the tender even knew they'd hit anything.

Ross put a hand to his head, and his fingertips encountered a swelling lump and a gash in the scalp that was bleeding freely and soaking his hair. He took careful inventory and was surprised to find the gash to be his only injury. He got to his feet. "Well, I'm alive," he muttered to himself. "But so are they."

Pulling out a bandanna, he wiped the moisture and blood from his face. "Well, Ross, old boy, what now?" For a man who hadn't expected to be alive, it was a problem he hadn't anticipated — getting through miles of enemy territory on foot to the safety of Union lines.

Chapter Thirteen
the reward of persistence

"Bust up that last car and set it afire!" J. J. Andrews stood on the forward ladder of the tender, looking back for any sign of their pursuers. The steady rain plastered his dark hair and trickled off his beard. But he seemed to be impervious to the weather, even though he was hatless in the hardest downpour of the day. "Get a good blaze going, boys. One of the Chicamauga bridges is less than three miles ahead."

The men in the one remaining boxcar jumped to obey. They couldn't assume Ross had successfully wrecked the pursuing train in the dark of Tunnel Hill. Carrick and the rest of the raiders knew firing this bridge might be their last chance to get away without having to turn and make a fight of it.

The men in the shelter of the boxcar fell to with fence posts, the one crowbar, and their bare hands to wrench what boards they could from the splintered walls. In the few minutes it took them to vent their frustrations, they wrecked the interior of the car, ripping large gaps in the sides and piling the loose wood in the middle of the floor. The remaining wood in the tender was soaked and only the roaring blaze in the firebox was hot enough to dry it sufficiently to burn. Not enough broken wood remained in the boxcar to run the engine for long, so Andrews was throwing everything they had into a last gamble.

When the boxcar was stripped of everything the men could tear loose, Knight passed the oilcan back, and they emptied the last of their precious supply onto the piled boards. Then Wilson carefully shoveled hot coals into a metal bucket and handed it to Andrews who passed it to Carrick and on down to the men in the boxcar. Fanned by the wind of their forward motion, the oil and coals quickly set the sheltered boards ablaze.

To Andrews's obvious satisfaction, the protected fire inside the boxcar flamed up and spread until the men, driven out by the smoke, crowded up into the tender. Two of them even climbed into the crowded cab.

Since passing the tunnel, their course trended northwest toward Ringgold and Chattanooga. The *General* angled across low, parallel ridges of land, dropping to run in the valleys for a distance, then climbing through low passes and down into the next valley.

Chickamauga Creek wound back and forth across their route, Josiah told Andrews. But Andrews apparently already knew this, because he planned to fire the first bridge over the creek. They were moving about thirty miles an hour, the slashing rain thoroughly wetting all the men in the open tender. Carrick had been careful not to lose his hat. It kept his head and neck relatively dry and comfortable. Several men from the boxcar were not so fortunate and just had to bow their heads and endure it, as they huddled inside the nearly empty tender. Sparks and wood ash from the balloon stack showered down on them, adding to the misery of the weather.

Carrick noticed that Mrs. Waymier appeared exhausted.

Her face was drawn and gray. She had slid to a sitting position in a corner of the cab, hugging her drawn-up knees. The man's clothing she wore was too big, making her seem to have shrunk inside it. Although he'd just met her today, Carrick felt sorry for her. If even only half the story she told was true, no wonder she was looking wan. From such stock, Josiah had inherited his confidence and tenacity.

Rounding a sweeping curve, they saw the first covered bridge over Chickamauga Creek. Knight slowed the *General*, and they stopped, positioning the boxcar in the middle of the bridge.

"Pull the pin and let's leave her," Andrews said to nobody in particular.

Carrick vaulted over the side and slid down the ladder. The blaze was leaping up and catching the dry inside walls and roof of the car. He turned his face from the heat, and stepped behind the tender to tug out the iron coupling pin. Given an hour or two, the fire would probably spread and grow large enough to catch the dry underside of the bridge covering, eventually destroying the whole structure. But they didn't have that much time. He flung the pin away in frustration, hearing it clatter hollowly against the boards of the bridge. They didn't even have fifteen minutes, he realized, as the wail of a distant steam whistle haunted them like a fearful, persistent ghost. Who would have thought, when this operation was being planned, that the weather would be the deciding element between success and failure? On a dry, breezy day, such as yesterday, they would have been well beyond pursuit by now, with at least one bridge connection severed behind them.

He climbed aboard the *General*, leaving the boxcar, and their last hope behind — a column of gray-white smoke pouring from the end of the covered bridge.

Within the next two miles, they crossed three more bridges over the same winding creek, but didn't pause. Andrews had played their last card. With no more fuel to attempt a fire, no more cross-ties to drop on the tracks, and no time to pull up a rail, it was now just a matter of trying to outrun pursuit to Chattanooga. The burning boxcar would not slow the Rebels down for long

Even though Knight did all he could, their speed gradually began to slacken. Andrews slipped off his overcoat, rolled it up, and tossed it into the firebox, along with the leather saddlebags he'd worn draped over an arm or shoulder since the beginning. Wilson glanced inquiringly at him, but he offered no explanation. Carrick guessed the bags contained forged letters and documents, possibly even written orders from the Union command that would have been fatally incriminating in the event of capture.

Carrick handed down the last of the wet wood from the tender, and Wilson shoved it in. There was nothing else to burn. The firebox door clanged shut on their hopes. Ringgold was near, but Chattanooga still another eighteen miles beyond that. Andrews and Wilson studied the steam pressure gauge, and the fireman shook his head, saying something Carrick couldn't hear. But Wilson's expression was clear. Perhaps they should have saved the broken boards from the last boxcar and used them for fuel. The raiders could always fight, but they weren't about to outrun anybody with no wood to make steam. At the rate the *General* was consuming wood, even that additional small amount would not have been enough. Carrick overheard Wilson also say the engine needed water.

The men in the tender were looking to their weapons, shielding the pistols from the flying mist with their hunched bodies. Since shedding his uniform, Carrick had almost stopped thinking of himself and the other men as soldiers. And Andrews, the spy, had never been in the military. But the men were now reacting as trained soldiers, preparing for battle with an enemy that was fast closing upon them. Without being told, everyone knew the end of the flight was near.

Carrick had nearly forgotten about the gold and silver, until he noted each man lugging his heavy ingot with him as he climbed into the tender. Like a drowning man hugging an anchor, he thought. Josiah Waymier sat on the footplate, sawing one of the yellow metal bars with the saw Scott had used to cut the telegraph wire. He ripped through the soft gold, sprinkling the iron deck with flecks of golden sawdust. Carrick watched him, fascinated, his attention temporarily distracted from their perilous situation.

"If we have to make a run for it, this won't be so heavy," Josiah said to his mother, handing her half an ingot. He shoved the other half into the side pocket of his coat, bulging and sagging the wool. His own gold bar lay untouched on the floor, alongside the extra bar Andrews had ordered for Amelia. Apparently Josiah was not giving up the idea of trying to escape with at least a little of the wealth his mother had worked so hard to secure. "Give these to the men," Josiah said, handing each of the extra ingots up to Carrick.

They rolled through the village of Ringgold, past the stone depot, ignoring the stares of local citizens. Beyond the town, the tracks formed a long curve and started a gradual upgrade. The *General*, starving for fuel, was laboring now, running about ten miles an hour. Only the smoke of the pursuing locomotive could be seen, but its whistle was growing ever louder.

"That's all she's got," Knight said as the *General* slowed

to the speed of a fast jog. They were about two miles north of Ringgold.

Still steaming in reverse, the *Texas* came into sight, pushing its tender. Apparently they had shunted the last burning boxcar onto a siding at Ringgold. Carrick guessed the pursuing engine was still well supplied with wood, but the Rebels had slowed to match their own speed. Carrick felt a thrill of savage delight as he realized the Confederates were fearful of closing with them.

"Are we going to fight?"

"No," Andrews replied.

The men muttered their astonishment, glancing curiously at one another. Many had pistols in hand. If Andrews had been an officer, Carrick thought, he would have commanded his men to defend themselves by force. But their leader was an undercover man, usually able to attain his goals by guile and subterfuge.

"We can't take on the whole Rebel force," Andrews added, glancing at Amelia Waymier, as if reluctant to expose her to gunfire. "It's every man for himself now. Jump off and scatter."

The locomotive was still chugging at ten miles an hour when the men began leaping off, some to the left and some to the right. The valiant *General* had brought them safely through almost ninety miles of enemy territory. She had given her best. But with no fuel and little water, she had now given her last.

"Let's go, Mother!" Josiah Waymier grabbed Amelia's hand and started for the right side of the cab.

Carrick quickly decided to go with them. He'd traveled on foot with Josiah before and now would help the young man protect his mother, whatever the cost to himself. A feeling of fatalism overtook him. "Off the left side into those woods!" he yelled at them. Josiah looked up, then he and Amelia moved to the other side of the cab. Eight of the men were already rolling on the ground, having jumped from the moving tender. He wondered why Knight didn't apply the brakes and stop. Just as he looked back, he saw Josiah's head disappear, followed quickly by his mother as they jumped from the chest-high footplate of the engine. He watched them tumble and roll down the embankment and held his breath, hoping the middle-aged woman was still strong and supple.

Three men were already scrambling up and crossing a rail fence, heading through a muddy field toward a line of trees.

Then Carrick saw why Knight hadn't stopped. The pursuing engine was accelerating, closing the gap. "Scattering like quail from a hunting dog," Carrick muttered to himself. "Damn!" He shoved his Remington back into its holster, knowing they would have a better chance by sticking together and fighting their pursuers. But Andrews had given the order, and now it was too late — raiders were running for their lives in several different directions.

It was time to act. He climbed over the side of the tender and held on for a second or two to pick out a landing place and gauge the speed of the engine. Then, hat in hand, he jumped forward and away from the train, tucking his shoulder and rolling as he struck the slope of the grassy embankment. He had more momentum than he realized and landed hard on his shoulder and back, knocking the wind out of himself, then cursed the stinging thistles that raked his face as he slid to a stop.

Leaping up, he looked to the Waymiers, scrambling to their feet twenty yards behind him. Josiah was helping his mother who appeared none the worse for her fall.

"This way!" Carrick ran toward them. Taking Amelia's

other arm, he helped lift her through a gap in the rail fence created by the men ahead of them.

Carrick glanced back once when he heard the crack of pistols. Puffs of white smoke came from four weapons being fired at them from the top of the tender fifty yards away. Two more men were in the locomotive cab. Carrick regretted Andrews's decision even more as he realized their own men outnumbered the Rebels behind them more than three to one.

But their main problem now lay in crossing the muddy wheat field and reaching the shelter of the woods on the other side. The saturated ground was soft, and, with every step, the mud clung to their boots, making their feet heavier and heavier. Carrick didn't know how many minutes passed; time seemed to slow to a standstill. No matter how much they struggled and panted and forced one foot ahead of the other, the trees were still two hundred yards away. Like a bad dream where something horrible was chasing him, he couldn't make his legs move to run.

Fuller would have joined his companions in firing at the fleeing raiders, but was not armed. Out of long habit for self-protection, he carried a small pocket pistol in his vest, opposite his watch, but rarely remembered to charge it with powder and shot. For several hours he'd been chasing this stolen train. Now that he'd caught up, the raiders were escaping into the woods, and, strangely enough, he didn't much care. Besides, on foot and in enemy territory, where could they go? The alarm had been given; they'd be rounded up soon enough.

His hatred of arrogant Yankees had been the spur that kept him going all day, forcing him onward when his body wanted to quit. But now that the *General* — *his* train — was in sight and barely moving, while the thieves were running away, he had a curious let-down. Somehow, in his imagination, these men had assumed a larger-than-life stature, always just out of view ahead, taunting him, obstructing his way with broken rails, cross-ties, burning boxcars, severed telegraph wires. They had taken on the mantle of gods, toying with his futile efforts to catch them. Now, as he watched them running for their lives through the muddy field, slipping, falling, obviously afraid, the whole picture deflated, and they became not only mere mortals, but just dirty, tired, frightened men. Let others take up the chase, he thought. He had his train back, the pride of his working life and the object of this exhausting pursuit. The raiders had failed; someone else could catch and punish the miscreants.

As the *Texas* chuffed slowly ahead, Fuller saw the engineer swing down from the *General*'s cab, the last man to leave the train. But he didn't leave it at a standstill. The engine was moving toward them in reverse with what little speed it still possessed.

Bracken braked the *Texas*, and then sent it slowly ahead, allowing the tender of the *General* to catch up and bump the tender of the *Texas*. Then he applied the brakes, and Fuller aided him by turning the brake wheel of the tender to bring both trains to a stop.

When Fuller mounted the cab of the captured locomotive, he found the firebox door open, and the fire burning low. The cocks showed the water level down.

"Did they do much damage?" Bracken asked, coming up.

"Not that I can see." Fuller glanced at three of the raiders who had nearly reached the trees on the far side of the wheat field.

"A brass journal overheated and melted," Bracken said.

"That can be fixed." Fuller rubbed his hand across the throttle handle. "Let's hook up and pull 'er back to Ringgold. We need to spread the word so those Yankee thieves can be rounded up. Most of our telegraph message from Dalton got through, so I reckon they'll dispatch some cavalry from Chattanooga to scour the countryside for 'em."

He pulled out his damp handkerchief to pad his hand and reached to close the iron firebox door. The light of the dying fire glinted off something on the footplate. He squatted to get a closer look. Tiny, glittering flecks adhered to his dampened fingertips, and he held them to the light of the dying fire.

"If that ain't gold, I'm a suck-egg mule," he muttered, glancing to see if Bracken was within earshot below the cab. *Where did that come from? Maybe this whole raid wasn't about burning bridges and disrupting our railroad, after all.*

He carefully raked up the remaining metallic particles, and folded them into his handkerchief. Should he make his discovery known to Bracken? Maybe later. This might be gold the raiders carried to buy necessities. But no one used gold dust any more. That was the medium of exchange in the gold fields and camps where coin and paper money were scarce. To keep from attracting attention to themselves before the raid, the thieves most likely would have used gold or silver coins or Confederate currency. Curious. Before he told anyone about this, he would look up an assayer and confirm his guess that it was actually gold.

He made a thorough search of the cab and the inside of the tender to see if anything else had been left. Not even one stick of wet wood remained. The raiders had gotten the maximum out of this engine before they fled on foot. Fuller grabbed the brass handles, and stepped down, feeling a surge of pride at having chased, and caught, the stolen locomotive. True, he could not have done it without a lot of help along the way, and some fortuitous circumstances. But that was the way the world worked — one did his best and then waited for fate to lend a hand.

"Let's hitch up. Then pull down about a half mile or so," Fuller said to Bracken. "I want to take a look along the roadbed to see if they threw out anything when they knew they were caught."

Bracken arched his eyebrows. "Like what?"

"You never know. These Yankees are a sneaky bunch."

Chapter Fourteen
Hounded

Amelia Waymier couldn't remember ever being so tired and dirty.

"Come on, Mother. We can't stop now," Josiah panted, pulling her arm.

They had just reached the edge of the woods and were looking back at the four men who were struggling across the open field after them.

"Josiah, let go of my arm! You're hurting me," she said irritably, jerking away from him.

"Sorry, but we have to keep going." He looked ahead at where three of the others were growing smaller in the dim green recesses of the forest.

"What those Rebs need is a little discouragement," Carrick said, drawing his Remington and taking aim at the nearest of the four men who was still a good sixty yards behind them. The pistol bucked and jumped in his hand, jetting a cloud of white smoke.

With a yell, one Rebel dived onto his belly in the mud and began firing back. The three other men scattered to make smaller targets.

Carrick fired twice more. "That'll give 'em something to think about." He smiled grimly. "They're civilians. Not used to being shot at." He turned to Amelia. "But Josiah's right. We can't stop here. Before long they'll have mounted men out searching for us."

She nodded, too short of breath to answer. Her boots were heavy with mud, and she tried vainly to scrape off some of it, using a small stick. Her arm bumped against a lump in the side pocket of her man's coat. Her half of the gold ingot. Should she cast it aside and lighten her load? She could hardly carry herself without dragging along this extra weight. "Let me . . . rest a minute . . . and catch my breath."

"We can rest later, unless you'd rather rest in a Reb prison," Josiah said, his youthful voice rising as he stared at the four men in the field behind them. "We need to get far enough ahead so we can find a place to hide. Then we can rest."

Amelia couldn't bear the thought of giving up or being captured. But her body and mind were at odds. She was used to hard work and her will was as strong as ever, yet her muscles refused to obey her commands. At fifty-two, she had just put herself through more mental and physical stress than she'd ever known, even in her younger years. She'd gone thirty-six hours without adequate sleep, while under the strain of deceiving the wagon guards, driving mules all night in the rain and mud, lifting heavy crates, then being jerked about on the fleeing locomotive. Even on the noisy, jolting engine, she'd nodded off several times while sitting on the floor of the cab.

She looked up at her son and found herself admitting that, even on her best day, she was not up to running with these men. They were a quarter century younger than she and had probably slept in a dry hotel the night before. She was finished, and she knew it.

"Go on without me," she said wearily. "Save yourself, Josiah. I'll stall them for you. Even Rebs won't hurt a woman. I'll make up some story that you kidnapped me. Here, take this gold."

"No, Mother! The wood yard man where you got aboard will tell them different. And they'll find out you stole the wagon at our house." Josiah gave Carrick a pained look. "We can't leave her."

"It never entered my mind," Carrick said briskly, firing one more shot at the four men who were on their feet again and coming toward them. A lead ball zipped through the leaves just above their heads as one of the men returned fire.

The bullet gave a surge of false energy to Amelia's tired limbs, and she struggled to her feet. She might have to surrender later, she thought, but it wouldn't be now, and it wouldn't be to those four idiots wildly chasing them.

With one man holding her under each arm, she started off at a half run, forcing her aching legs to perform when all they wanted to do was let the rest of her body fall to the ground like some great, dead weight and rest . . . rest. . . . The men lifted and propelled her along, her feet sometimes not even touching the ground.

She didn't know how long they ran, or in what direction. Being half carried, her windmilling legs tried to keep pace with the long strides of her son and this soldier. She was in a daze, numbly fading in and out for the next hour, or the next century. Time and reality had slipped a cog or two.

Finally she came fully alert again as they set her down on a grassy spot under some tall trees. The men were gasping like fish out of water. At least, they were sheltered from the rain. She could hear rain falling hard on the overhead leaves. No, that wasn't rain. That was the sound of rushing water. They were near a stream of some kind.

"Chickamauga Creek," Josiah gasped, as if in reply to her unasked question.

"Running high and fast with all this rain," Carrick added.

"The creek makes a lot of loops around through here," Josiah said. "I'm not all that familiar with the terrain this far from the right-of-way."

"Which way is west?" Amelia asked.

Carrick looked around as if trying to get his bearings. He finally pointed across the creek. "I think that way."

"We'd be better off going west," she said, her voice sounding weak in her own ears. "Maybe pass south of Chattanooga. Aren't the Federal forces somewhere near Bridgeport, Alabama?"

Carrick nodded, taking deep breaths. "But we'd have to cross Look-Out Mountain on foot. Even if we could do it, we'd have a tough time keeping to the right direction with no sun or compass. We'd have to travel at night."

Both men were still panting and didn't speak for a minute. "But we should probably try to get up into the mountains and find a place to rest," Carrick finally said. "It would be impossible for horsemen to come into the heavy woods and underbrush on the steep mountainsides."

Each man had sunk to one knee, catching his breath, facing Amelia who sat on the wet grass. She was beginning to get her second wind, when a distant sound sent a chill up her back — the far-off baying of hounds!

Her heart began to race. They exchanged startled glances.

"Not likely they're out looking for runaway slaves," Carrick said, standing up and flexing his back.

"We need to put the creek between us and them," Josiah

replied. "Maybe throw 'em off the scent."

Amelia looked at the dark water of the creek roaring along, at least twenty yards wide and very swift. Her stomach contracted. Even if they could find a ford, it would be at flood now. She had been a good swimmer as a girl and young woman, but that had been many years ago. This was an entirely different situation. She had never tested herself against such a wild current. "This might prove worse than what's behind us," Amelia said, trying to hide her uneasiness. She had no fear of men, since she understood human nature and had dealt with all kinds of people in her lifetime. But the impersonal forces of nature sometimes appalled and frightened her. She had been able to ignore the ferocity of the storm at her home because she'd used it to her advantage to help cover the theft of the wagon. But this raging creek could drag her away. The thought of suffocating under the dark, cold water brought on near panic.

The bloodhounds started baying again. Was her fear making them sound closer?

"They've either got our scent, or they're being held in check so the men can keep up," Carrick said. "Otherwise, the dogs would be running quietly."

"Let's go," Josiah said, stripping off his jacket. "I'll go first. The current will drift us down a ways, but that's even better. Our scent will stay on top of the water, and the hounds could detect it if this were a pond or some still water. As it is, they'll be delayed picking up our trail if we don't come out just opposite this spot." He handed Carrick his pistol and powder flask. "Keep this dry."

He waded into the edge of the stream. When the water reached his waist, he struck off, swimming. Amelia held her breath as she saw the current sweep her youngest son downstream like a stick of wood, only his head bobbing above the surface. But he struck off in a strong sidestroke, and, before he'd been carried more than forty yards, he was standing up on the bottom, wading out on the far shore. He waved that he was all right and signaled for them to come ahead.

"Here, I'll help you," Carrick said. "Give me your coat."

"It's got half a gold ingot in the pocket," she replied, handing him the soggy wool jacket. "Maybe I should just throw it away or hide it under a log somewhere."

"No." He shook his head. "We might need it later if we have to buy food or bribe someone to hide us."

She hadn't thought that far ahead. Apparently Gibson Carrick was not anticipating capture. He was an undercover soldier who'd been in this situation before. She wondered briefly about him. Was he a native Southerner? Very likely. Giving family names for first names was a Southern custom. Maybe he came from one of the many families with divided loyalties in this war.

Carrick quickly put his Remington and Josiah's Colt Navy in the other side pocket of her coat and rolled it up.

"Should I take off these boots?" she asked. "They're so wet, I don't know if I can get them off . . . or back on."

"No. You might lose them. Don't worry, the current is swift, but that's to our advantage. It'll help buoy us up."

"I can swim," she said. "I don't need to hold onto you. Just stay close in case I get into trouble."

"All right. Here we go." He took her hand, and they waded in.

She gasped as the icy water reached her thighs. They struck off side-by-side. The black torrent seemed to engulf her and took her breath. Some of the water slopped into her mouth and nose, and she coughed and gagged.

"Don't fight it," Carrick warned from a few feet away.

"Just keep stroking and angle across. Let the current do the work."

She concentrated on relaxing, expending only the amount of effort necessary to stay afloat and gain a few feet every couple of strokes. She could see Carrick out of the corner of her eye, holding her coat above his head with one hand while he swam with the other.

He was right. If it hadn't been for the swift current, her water-logged pants and boots would surely have dragged her under. She fought down an instinctive panic and forced her mind to focus on relaxing and pulling herself across with a steady sidestroke.

After what seemed like hours, her boots struck the gravel bottom and Josiah was pulling her up on shore. Her heavy clothes streamed cold water, but she felt warmed a little by her exertions.

As she pulled on her damp coat, she saw they were in a worse spot than before. They were in a bend where the current swung wide and had cut a nearly vertical mud bank a dozen feet high. The bank stretched in both directions as far as she could see.

"We don't want to follow the creek," Carrick said. "We need to go straight away from it and put as much distance as possible between us and those dogs."

Easier said than done, she thought.

"I think that's west." Josiah gestured at the steep bank in front of them. "This is the next obstacle, and we can't be wasting any time looking for a way around it. Think you can climb it?" he asked his mother.

"I'll try," Amelia said. "If I can swim that creek, this shouldn't be any worse." She tried to sound confident, but inside she quailed at the thought of falling back into the rushing water.

"Let me go first," Carrick said. "Then Amelia."

Amelia followed him up the steep bank, trying to step and reach where he did, her boots slipping and sliding as she attempted to dig her toes into the soft dirt. Hand holds were scarce — only a few projecting rock ledges and some scrawny bushes still clinging by their roots. Her legs ached fearfully and her breath came in labored gasps as she struggled upward.

Twice she slipped back, colliding with her son. But he checked her fall and gave her a boost to get started again. She was not as young and strong as these men, but was determined not to show weakness. Come what may, she would not be responsible for slowing down their flight. In a moment of depression, she had earlier offered to give up and let them go on. But they'd refused, as she knew they would. Now she would give her dying effort until she could go no farther. If it came to the point where she had to be carried, she would insist they leave her. But for now, the baying of the distant hounds injected a thrill of fear that gave life to her limbs. Stealing their gold and their train was not something these Rebels would take lightly. She could not depend on them to be genteel in their treatment of a woman prisoner — especially when they found out she'd lived in the South for years and had betrayed them. She didn't even want to imagine what her jailers would do if she had been young and beautiful.

As she neared the top, her mind was occupied by other things. She failed to test the stability of a bush before putting her weight on it. The roots pulled loose. She gave a startled yell and lost her balance. She felt her body slam into Josiah, but, once again, he saved her from falling. Both slid back about six feet before they could grip the slimy bank with hands and knees and arrest their slide.

"Are you all right?" she asked, clinging to a rock and not daring to look down.

"Yes."

She could hear him spitting dirt out of his mouth.

"I'm sorry I yelled."

"It's all right. Nobody near enough to hear," he said. "Up we go again. Take it easy, now. Make sure of every move. Just keep looking up," he encouraged her.

Finally she felt Carrick pulling her arm nearly out of its socket as he reached down from level ground and heaved her up with one mighty yank.

With no food or rest, their reserves of stamina were severely depleted. All three lay on the ground gasping for several minutes before they regained enough strength to get up and move on. Amelia felt better, seeing that she was not the only one near exhaustion. But the younger men would recover more quickly, so she had to conserve her energy to keep up.

Even though the rain fell steadily, they were somewhat protected by the heavy forest canopy. The gray overcast prevented them from judging any accurate directions by the sun. She guessed it was probably early to mid-afternoon. But the dark day, blending with the wet, green foliage all blurred in her tired brain as they walked and sometimes ran, away from the creek, trying to keep a straight course up and down the low hills. A pocket compass would have been a great help, but who would have anticipated needing one?

When she began to fall behind, Josiah slowed to help her along. She lost track of time, but it was perhaps an agonizing half hour later when they came to a long, sloping meadow that ran uphill several hundred yards, ending in some rather open woods on a mountainside.

They paused at the low edge of the meadow, breathing

heavily, just inside the cover of the trees.

"Listen!" Josiah panted.

Over their own harsh breathing, she could hear shouting in the distant woods somewhere off to their right. Then three gunshots blasted the afternoon stillness.

"They're hot on the trail of something," Carrick said.

"Sounds like a lot of men," Amelia replied. "But only four got off that train behind us."

"It's muster day," Josiah said, "and I saw a bunch of cavalry as we passed through Ringgold."

"You can bet all the men and boys, who are able to hold a gun, are out tramping the woods to run down the train thieves," Carrick said. "They've riled up all the local citizens to hunt us down like rabid animals."

Gone was any thought Amelia had of surrender. From the sounds, she feared that these furious farmers and citizens would be in no mood to take prisoners. Their blood lust was up enough that they might shoot on sight.

"With all that shooting, they must have spotted some of the boys," Josiah panted.

"At least, I don't hear any dogs," Amelia said.

"They're not moving fast enough to be on horseback," Carrick added. "We need to get across this field and up into the woods on that mountainside," he continued. "If we keep to the high ground and thick woods, I think our chances are better."

"They're coming closer." Amelia nodded toward the noise. "They'll see us if we try to cross this field. I don't think I can run that fast."

"We don't have time to cross," Carrick said, looking around. "Over here! A place to lie down and hide until they pass." He led the way to a big tree that had been cut down some months before. The limbs had been chopped off and lay in heaps around the huge log, and dead leaves still clung to the branches, forming a big, tangled pile.

"Slide in under there and I'll cover you," he directed Josiah. "Be ready to come out shooting in case we're discovered. They'll be in sight within a minute."

While Josiah was hiding, Amelia squirmed in under the brush heaped on the other side of the downed tree, and Carrick adjusted the branches over her. Peeking through the leaves, she saw Carrick draw his Remington and check the priming, then crawl in under the wet brush. They all lay still. She couldn't see either man, and prayed that the casual observer would not give the piles of dead brush a second glance.

The crashing and snapping of twigs and undergrowth grew louder as the hunters approached. Amelia froze, holding her breath, but her heart was hammering in her ears.

"Where the hell did they get to?" a man yelled so close that she started. "I had two of 'em in sight."

Amelia tried to become part of the log.

"You made enough noise to scare off half the Yankee Army," another said.

Out of the corner of her eye, she could see a pair of booted legs standing within two feet of her. A musket barrel swung down beside her. Then her wet clothes began to itch. She gritted her teeth in agony. If she stirred an inch, they'd be discovered.

"Ya hafta make a little noise if you're gonna scare up the game."

Amelia could see this man clearly through the leaves as he spat out a wad of tobacco and wiped the inside of his mouth with a grimy forefinger.

"Maybe we oughta get more help," another voice said,

out of Amelia's sight.

"You skeered of 'em, Mort?"

"Hell, they've got guns, too. One of 'em took a shot at me."

"Huh! More'n likely it was old Eben who shot at ya," the first man replied. "He's bringing up the rear, and shoots at anything that moves. Damned glad he ain't got a repeater, or he'd bag us all."

Someone gave a snort of derisive laughter, and the men walked right past the downed tree and the brush pile where the fugitives lay hidden. Amelia was in a panic for fear they could hear her breathing, but the men were making so much noise, they drowned every other sound.

"Let's spread out and see if we can pick up their trail. They didn't cross this field or we would've seen 'em. You and Mort go back into the woods on that side and we'll run on ahead and duck into the woods up about a hundred yards. And, for God's sake, don't be shootin' at us! Give a shout if you spot 'em."

The men continued to yell back and forth as three of them passed within four feet of Amelia's hiding place. She thought she would explode if she couldn't scratch.

Chapter Fifteen
hunger

After an eternity, the voices and footsteps moved away, receding as they continued the hunt. When the sounds finally faded into the distance, Amelia turned toward Carrick, catching his eye as he raised his head cautiously above the fallen log. He motioned for her to keep quiet and lie still. Fifteen more minutes crept by and the sounds disappeared altogether as the manhunters passed over the crest of a hill.

Josiah crawled cautiously out of his hiding place, and the three of them crouched on the low side of the fallen tree. Amelia squirmed and rubbed all the itchy places. She fervently wished she could strip off these soggy clothes and pull on something dry next to her skin.

"Not the kind of rabble you want after you," Carrick said. "I'd much rather it be regular cavalry. At least they'd have some military discipline and not be likely to shoot us on the spot."

"I thought sure I'd have to come out shooting," Josiah said, his light complexion looking even paler. "One of them nearly stepped on my hand."

"We'll use our guns only as a last resort to defend ourselves," Carrick said. "But we *will* escape."

For a few moments they all paused, gathering their own

thoughts and feelings.

"These manhunters are thicker than ticks," Carrick said. "We'd best lie low right here until dark. If I'm any judge, those hayseeds will get tired and wet and hungry and go home for a hot meal by then, whether or not they catch anyone. Tonight we'll head up into the mountains."

"Do you reckon they got a telegraphic message through to Chattanooga before Scott cut the wire that last time?" Josiah wondered aloud.

"Very possible," Carrick said, "because they were pressing us pretty hard at Dalton."

"What will happen if they did?" Amelia asked.

"Confederate cavalry will be sent to sweep the area. Men on horseback can cover a lot of ground in a short time. That's why I want to get up into the steep mountains . . . Missionary Ridge or Look-Out Mountain. It will be hard going for us on foot, but it will be impossible on horseback, especially at night."

Amelia looked at this soldier who had befriended her son and her. He was close to thirty, she guessed, and obviously more physically mature and experienced than Josiah. There was something familiar about the black mustache and his confident air. Then it dawned on her that Carrick reminded her of her absent son, Albert, Jr., who'd gone to Mexico this past year. Would she ever see him again in this world? The terrible war had made all their lives precarious. From day to day, even moment to moment, nothing was certain as far as their human minds knew. Yet, she believed that everything was certain, was pre-ordained. The choices they made, the choices their enemies made — would all mesh into some inevitable conclusion that was known to the Creator from eternity. She had always accepted predestination as a fact. But given time really to ponder it, she had some trouble wrapping her mind around the concept. Perhaps there was a difference between *knowing* the future, and *causing* it.

Amelia was hungry, but her hunger was not a gnawing pain. The last food she'd eaten was the snack of cold fried chicken and biscuits she'd packed and consumed early this morning while waiting for the train near Cartersville.

"When did you last eat?" she asked Josiah.

He paused, as if this were the last question he'd expected. "Late yesterday on the way down to Marietta," he answered. "We had a supper stop. Seems like a week ago."

She nodded.

"Are you hungry?" he asked solicitously.

"Not too bad," she said. "More tired than anything. No sleep last night. Wish I had some dry clothes."

"You still think we should stay here until nightfall?" Josiah asked.

"Absolutely," Carrick answered. "I know we're all wet and hungry. But we're free and we're armed. After this first flush of excitement dies down, we'll be much safer traveling, especially after dark." He busied himself scraping out a more comfortable hiding place under the branches from where he'd just emerged. "We don't want to lose patience. We can outlast and outsmart these people until we get away from here. Even though it's been up and down hill, I doubt if we're more than three miles in a direct line from the railroad." He embraced both of them with a cheerful smile. "Our bodies will warm these wet clothes a little. You can bet we'd be a lot more miserable in a Rebel prison. So, if you can ignore being uncomfortable, snug down out of sight and get a good nap. Those hunters won't be back this way because they've already covered this ground and have satisfied themselves that nobody's here. We can relax as long as we stay out of sight and keep quiet."

Amelia seemed to draw strength and confidence from her older son's look-alike. When she was bone-weary, all problems seemed insurmountable. She just needed someone to assure her that everything was going to be all right. Carrick had done just that.

She crawled back in under the thick branches. Carrick made sure she was covered. Using her arm for a pillow, she closed her eyes, and a terrible weariness overcame her.

As she was beginning to rise from the deep sleep of exhaustion, she heard the rustling of paper nearby. Where was she? She opened her eyes wide. Blackness. She rolled over and felt the stiffness of her body in the damp clothing. Then she remembered, and wished she could go back to sleep again, to regain the blissful oblivion. The rustling sounded again. It was the soft crackling of dry brush — not paper. Gibson Carrick was stirring nearby.

"It's time to be up and moving," he said softly.

Amelia rolled out into the open, and sat up. She could barely make out his bulky form moving in the darkness several feet away.

"Oohh!" Josiah groaned.

She heard her son's voice from the other side of the big, downed tree. He'd always been a heavy sleeper, even as a boy, and was usually grumpy when awakened. Apparently he was suffering from the same stiffened muscles that afflicted them all.

"What time is it?" he asked.

"My watch got wet and stopped," Carrick answered, holding the timepiece to a shaft of moonlight filtering through the overhead branches. "But I'd guess about eight or half past."

Amelia got to her feet with a muffled groan, but was

grateful that the spring rain had finally stopped and the moon was shining. She'd slept at least five hours, maybe more. As achy, damp, and uncomfortable as she was, she felt better and stronger for the sleep. Her heavy limbs had been lightened, her flagging spirit restored to a great degree. She felt the need to urinate and excused herself, retreating deeper into the woods. Even though it was dark, she found an oak tree with a trunk large enough to shield her. While partially disrobed, she rubbed her damp skin vigorously to help restore circulation and warmth to the surface of her thighs and buttocks. The clothing next to her skin had begun partially to dry from body heat while she slept, but it would be a long time, she reflected, before the cotton would be anywhere near comfortable. She wondered how men could stand to wear pants all the time.

As she returned, ready to go, she reflected that she hadn't allowed excess flesh to accumulate with the years. If she could toughen herself to these rigors of travel, she had no doubt she would survive this ordeal.

"We're lucky the moon is out," Carrick said. "That should help keep us on some sort of straight course. Let's go."

They struck off at a fast walk across the upland meadow, the wet grass shining in the pale light. It was a beautiful sight and Amelia felt good about their chances. She had awakened hungry. Steady, cross-country travel might bring them to a house or cabin where they could beg food. But Carrick had warned that they must put several more miles behind them before attempting to find something to eat. They had to get beyond the range of the manhunters who'd probably alerted the country people to the raiders' presence.

Once they reëntered the woods, the heavy forest canopy

effectively shut out any moonlight. Only here and there a shaft of light penetrated. Carrick, taking the lead, guided them, and she fell in behind him. Josiah brought up the rear. She hoped they were traveling in a straight line away from the dangers behind them — especially from the men with the hounds.

The big trees had apparently shaded out much of the undergrowth. Even so, they were continuously stumbling over or crawling under windfalls, shielding their faces from stickers as they forced their way through wet blackberry thickets.

"Can't you find us a smoother path?" Amelia finally panted.

"Sorry. Wish I could," Carrick replied. "But we've lost the moon and I'm trying to follow as straight a course as I can. If I start detouring around these obstacles, I'll lose what little sense of direction I have."

During the next two hours, they stopped to rest three times. By now Amelia's legs had begun to ache with the strain of walking uphill. As the night wore on, their plodding fell into a routine. It seemed they had been crashing along through this dark, wet forest for eternity. She automatically followed two or three paces behind Carrick, one heavy boot thudding after another, and her mind began to wander. Were they ascending the steep parapet that was Missionary Ridge, just south of Chattanooga? She tried to call up a mental picture of a map of this area. She'd never had reason to study a map of the terrain in detail, so had only a vague notion of what it looked like. Now she was encountering the reality of the rugged, steep, forested mountainsides. If they traveled almost due west from where they'd abandoned the train, they would parallel the Georgia-Tennessee state line a few miles south of Chattanooga — a town they wanted to avoid at all costs, since it was currently filled with regiments of the Rebel Army. If they could somehow scale the escarpment of Look-Out Mountain — no mean feat, even in daylight with plenty of food and rest — they would eventually come close to Bridgeport, Alabama on a bend of the Tennessee River. Here, it was rumored, General Mitchell occupied the place with Union troops. This was the shortest route to the Union lines — and probably the most difficult.

Every hour or two, Amelia shifted the chunk of gold from one side pocket of her jacket to the other. She wished they had the means of cutting the ingot once again so it would be in two lighter pieces, easier to handle and carry.

In the black hours before daylight, she lost all track of time. Her mind almost slept while her body kept swinging forward in a steady rhythm. As if in a dream, she saw flashes of mules plunging ahead of her in the dark rain, felt the heavy wagon slipping in the mud, her struggles to control the team. This picture faded, and she saw herself sitting on the footplate of the locomotive, heat nearly withering the side of her face every time Wilson swung open the firebox door. She felt herself being flung from side to side against the bruising iron and metal levers, the big engine roaring as it lunged ahead.

Carrick stopped suddenly, and she thudded against him. He turned and caught her as her knees suddenly buckled. She shook her head and stood upright. Gray daylight was seeping through the forest canopy.

"There's a cabin ahead," Carrick said in a hoarse whisper.

She and Josiah crowded up to look. In the dim, early morning she could see a small log house in a shallow mountain cove about a hundred yards distant. A rough, whipsawed barn with a dogtrot stood thirty yards to one side and a few smaller outbuildings were scattered around.

"No smoke from the chimney and no animals in sight. Either the people aren't up yet, or nobody's home," Carrick observed.

"I wonder if that barn has some dry horse blankets or something to sleep on?" Amelia said.

"Just what I was thinking," Carrick agreed. "But we'll have to hurry. It's getting daylight. We'll circle around in the woods and come up to the barn from the back. Keep the outbuildings between us and the house."

Fifteen minutes later they approached the barn from the rear, quietly slipped into the dogtrot. Several chickens scratched and pecked in the straw beside a dusty buggy.

Amelia jerked her head around at a slight movement, then saw a bay horse rubbing against the door of a stall.

"Well, at least we know the place is occupied," Josiah whispered.

"Up there," Carrick said, pointing to the loft.

The three of them climbed the wooden ladder, and Amelia sighed at the sight of the huge pile of clean-looking hay.

"We'll sleep here today," Carrick said. "Maybe tonight we can beg some food from the folks in that house, then move on."

Amelia had already pulled off the soggy wool coat and was burrowing down into the fresh-smelling hay. The men wasted no time selecting places to do the same.

"Be sure to cover up completely," came Carrick's voice from a few feet away. "We should be safe enough here, if we stay quiet." He thrust his head up from where he'd hollowed out a nest. "Do either of you snore?"

Amelia tried to stifle a laugh but then she saw he was serious. "Not loud enough to be heard more than a few feet away," she said with a grin. She tugged off her boots and wet socks and vigorously rubbed her wrinkled white feet. Then she settled into the blissfully comfortable hay. It seemed softer than any feather tick she'd ever slept in. Her last thought before she drifted away was of the mice that might be sharing her sleeping quarters. But she was really beyond caring.

Amelia swam up from the depths of a heavy sleep to the rustling of someone stirring nearby. Her drowsy mind told her it was one of the men. Why was he making so much noise? She was on the verge of whispering for him to be quiet, when a woman's voice said: "I wish Bill would cobble together a chicken coop for these hens. But he never seems to find the time. Makes it mighty hard to hunt all over creation to find their eggs."

Another woman, much closer, said: "Here's a hole. I wouldn't wonder if there's a nest in here."

Amelia was wide awake now and holding her breath. There was a scuffing sound as the woman thrust her hand down inside the dent in the hay.

A scream filled the space under the barn roof. Then another. And the sound of scrambling bodies. "There's someone here!" came the hysterical screech.

Raising her head just enough, Amelia saw two women tripping on their long dresses as they floundered through the soft hay to the ladder. There was a *thud* as one of them jumped, or fell, to the packed earth below.

"Oh! My God! My God! He was alive!" The panicked voice receded with the running footsteps.

Amelia's heart was racing as she crawled out to see Carrick looking at her. "Rotten luck!" he said. "She reached in and happened to touch my bare hand."

"Enough to scare a body out of a year's growth," Amelia said with feeling. Her own heart rate was beginning to slow.

Yellow yolk of a broken egg streaked one of the ladder's upright posts. Three brown eggs lay unbroken in the hay, and Amelia retrieved them, placing them gently in her coat pocket.

"If there're any men in that house, they'll be up here with guns in about a minute," Carrick said. "Let me do the talking. We'll try to bluff our way through."

"What's all the ruckus about?" Josiah grunted, finally rolling up, his eyes heavy with sleep.

Amelia shook her head. "How do you ever stand sentry duty?"

He looked at her, as if trying to grasp her question, or her sarcasm. "I don't go to sleep," he finally answered.

"Make sure to keep those chunks of gold out of sight," Carrick said, looking around for his hat.

Amelia picked pieces of hay out of her hair and made a vain attempt at brushing off her clothes. "Wish I had a mirror," she said.

When more than three minutes had passed and no sound came from the cabin, Carrick said: "We may be in luck. Those women might be alone."

Amelia pulled on her wet boots with some difficulty, and the three dirty refugees descended the ladder. They paused in the dogtrot.

"I think our best bet is to go up to the house and apologize for scaring them. Whatever story I start, you can back me up," Carrick said. "Anybody have a better idea?"

"Nope," Josiah said.

Amelia shook her head. She felt much more rested, even though hunger pangs were beginning to trouble her. The angle of the sun above the hills told her it was past mid-afternoon.

"Did they see you?" Carrick asked Amelia as they approached the porch.

"Don't believe so."

"I wish they had. Seeing another woman would not be nearly as terrifying as finding just three rough-looking men in the barn."

They stepped up onto the porch, and he rapped briskly on the plank door.

Silence. He rapped again. The door was opened a crack, and an older woman put one eye around the edge. "Yeh?"

Carrick, holding his hat in both hands, said: "Ma'am, I'm very sorry we frightened you. We were out chasing those train thieves and got caught in the rain late last night. We didn't want to disturb anyone at that hour, so we just took shelter in your barn to sleep."

Amelia saw the woman's gaze flick past Carrick to her, then to Josiah.

"We're awfully hungry and would be glad to pay you for something to eat," Amelia added.

Apparently the sound of a woman's voice decided the issue. After a moment's hesitation, the door swung inward, and she stepped back to admit them. Amelia watched the younger woman, standing behind the door, lower her double-barreled shotgun and ease down the hammers. These two women might be alone, she thought, but they were far from helpless.

"We got some cold buttermilk from the spring house and some leftover cornbread," the older woman said. "You're welcome to it. "We would 'a' had eggs, too, but. . . ."

"Here's three good ones I found," Amelia said, holding them out with a smile.

This seemed to break the remaining tension. "Thankee kindly," the middle-aged woman said. "My name's Ruth Starnes," she added. "This is my niece, Mary Mason."

Amelia nodded, and Carrick introduced them all by false names. Amelia made a mental note that henceforth she was Bess White. But she forgot everything else when they sat down to eat. As the meal progressed, she was able to loosen the belt a notch.

Amelia noticed the two women still staring at them suspiciously, as if they couldn't figure out why a graying, middle-aged woman would be out, dressed in male attire, tramping the rainy woods in search of some train thieves.

"I was up from Cartersville, visiting my son in Ringgold, when all that excitement about the stolen train came about," she explained around a mouthful of food. "We decided to join the search."

The two women nodded their understanding, but didn't speak.

Amelia thought she'd never tasted anything so delicious in her life as that cornbread and buttermilk. The younger woman, watching them devour everything she set before them, hastened to bring out some cold sweet potatoes to add to the fare.

As they ate, Amelia let her eyes take in the room. Other than the flower print curtains at the windows, the rather primitive cabin lacked any amenities. No table cloth, only tinware to eat from, no rugs on the puncheon floor. A subsistence farm, if she'd ever seen one.

When they finished, Amelia was still not full, but she felt much better. They dared not ask for more, wanting to appear only hungry, not starved.

"I hope we haven't eaten the supper you fixed for your

men folk," Carrick said, handing her some damp, folded Confederate bills.

"The men are. . . ."

"We got more," the older Ruth interrupted her niece quickly. "Our husbands are off hunting. They'll be back afore sundown."

Two women alone and scared in these mountains, Amelia immediately deduced. She could empathize with that. The men were probably either off to war, or working for wages in Chattanooga to supplement their meager existence. "We been tramping around in the dark in these woods and kinda got turned around," she said in a friendly manner. "Can you point the way to Chattanooga?"

"You ain't but five miles east by south from town," Ruth answered.

Amelia had to duck her head to hide her disappointment. She had felt sure they were several miles west of Chattanooga by now. It seemed they'd been walking forever, but, apparently, they'd been going more north than west.

"We won't trouble you ladies any more," Carrick said quickly, as the three of them shuffled out the door. In case they were being watched, they stepped off down the rutted wagon road that led north through the cove in the direction of Chattanooga.

When they were well out of sight, they ducked off the road into the woods, moving again toward the setting sun. They'd hardly gone twenty yards, when they heard the sounds of horses coming down the road they'd just vacated. Crouching behind some bushes, they could hear snatches of conversation from the half dozen men who rode by. Manhunters. Amelia wondered if the horsemen had gotten any information from the two women at the cabin.

As a precaution, they hid themselves in a thicket until dusk. Then they held a conference and decided to abandon their plan of trying to walk straight west over the mountains toward Alabama. Without sufficient food, rest, and dry clothing, they felt the mighty escarpment of Look-Out Mountain would be too much for them to surmount. Amelia wondered if the men voted to change their plans for her sake. Nothing was said to this effect, but she suspected her age and lack of physical stamina probably influenced their decision.

"Feels like we've already walked forty miles," Carrick said, shaking his head. "Those two women said we're still east of Chattanooga. It's my fault we've been wandering all over the place. Our best chance now is to head north for the Tennessee River and find a boat. Maybe we can slip past 'em by water."

Whatever the reasoning, Amelia was glad of the change. They were still in rough country, but the night was clear, and they were able to pick out the North Star to help maintain their direction.

Carrick led the way. An hour or so after full dark, he stopped suddenly. Before Amelia could ask what was wrong, she heard voices only a few yards away.

"Gimmie a light offen your pipe," a gravely voice said.

She froze in her tracks, as did Josiah behind her.

There was silence for several seconds. She saw a pinpoint of light nearby and caught a whiff of tobacco smoke. "You reckon it's time for our relief yet?" the same voice asked.

Someone coughed and spat. "Not likely. It just *seems* like we been out here a week," the other man replied. There was an interval of silence. "Road guard is a mighty tiresome business," the first man said. "Do they really think the Yanks are going to be marchin' down this back road in the middle of the night?"

"The Army does things by routine, not by logic," the other sentry replied. "This may be boring, but it sure beats gettin' your head shot off in some battle."

"Reckon so. . . ."

The voices trailed off as Carrick carefully guided Amelia and Josiah in a wide circle around the two sentries. She was aware of her heart pounding. It had been a near thing.

Through occasional gaps in the trees she was startled at first by the sight of a big, orange light, then realized it was only a full moon rising. It climbed into the night sky and provided them with sufficient light, even in the woods, to see where they were going. Now there was a lot less tripping and stumbling. Amelia had plenty of time to wonder if nights spent sleeping really contained as many hours as nights spent hiking through forests.

By dawn they found themselves well concealed in heavy timber at the foot of the mountain. Through a break in the trees, they watched the rising of the sun, and stepped into a clearing to enjoy its warmth. It cheered Amelia like an old friend. She felt her spirits rising after the many days of rain. Her clothes were nearly dry. She pulled off her boots and massaged her feet.

Then they concealed themselves in a thicket and slept the day through. The mosquitoes had not yet made an appearance. Perhaps the spring chill kept them at bay.

When darkness fell, they started out again and spent another long night, struggling over rocks, feeling their way down steep slopes and through undergrowth. Amelia tried to put her mind on other things. She calculated that this was Tuesday night. The train had been stolen on Saturday.

All that seemed so long ago! She wondered how many of the raiding party were still on the loose.

Wednesday morning found them still among the mountains, but as soon as the sun was warm enough, they prepared to lie down in a protected area among some rocks for a nap.

"I'm about to starve!" Amelia said, looking at Josiah and Carrick, who had not complained. She supposed they were trying to act manly, but she noticed her son's face was paler than before and had a pinched look about it. This hurt her more than her own hunger. She could stand to lose a few pounds, she admitted to herself, but his spare frame could ill afford the loss.

She sat on the ground, and carefully spread her dirty socks on a rock in the sun. Even though they and the boots were dry, the man's boots were too large for her and were beginning to rub blisters, in spite of her care. It was something she'd been dreading. As long as they had to hike, she had been particular about taking care of her feet. She had even torn off part of her dry shirt tail and carefully wrapped strips of cotton around her toes and heels to prevent chafing. So far, so good, even though two blisters were on the verge of forming. Plenty of air and sunlight on her feet would help.

"There's no sign of people," Josiah said. "Don't you think we'd be safe traveling in the daylight?"

Carrick nodded, looking at Amelia. "If your mother's up to it."

"I'm game for a few more hours," she said, starting to redress her feet. As she stood up, she noticed how slack her pants were about her hips. She pulled the belt up another notch. "Let's go."

They pushed on with a false energy, hoping to locate

some kind of food. It was too early in the year even to find ripe berries.

Guided by the sun, they pushed northeastward, and by mid-afternoon came out on the brow of a hill overlooking a picturesque mountain valley, thickly dotted with houses. It was a lovely sight. They stood for a long minute, drinking in the peace and beauty of the place below them. The more Amelia looked, the more the little valley appeared to be a corner of paradise. Her imagination conjured up pictures and aromas of stew and cornbread and chicken and dumplings. They had not eaten for forty-eight hours.

"Boys," she announced, sitting down on the grass, "I'm not going another mile without some food."

"Yeah, we could starve in these mountains just as easily as we could in a Confederate jail," Josiah said. "Let's take a chance and try that little cabin right below us. It's set off away from the others."

"There's smoke coming from the chimney," Carrick added, "so there's likely something cooking."

"I'll make up some story," Carrick said, as he began searching for a way down. "But be ready for anything, just in case." He loosened the Remington in its holster.

Amelia got to her feet. She felt as weak and stiff as a ninety-year-old, and had to hold onto her son as they descended the steep hill to whatever awaited them in the log house below.

Chapter Sixteen

a bright spot in the darkness

A young woman answered their knock.

"Ma'am, we got lost in the mountains and are really hungry," Carrick said in his most civil and subservient tone. "We'd be mighty obliged if you could give us something to eat. We'll gladly pay you," he added.

"Most assuredly," she said, as if she'd been waiting for them all day. "Come in."

Amelia was immediately at ease. Maybe it was intuition, but this woman seemed the most open and generous, the least suspicious of anyone she'd met in some time. She was a tall, buxom woman of about thirty, black hair, short fingernails, and callused hands as if used to hard work. She wore a long gray flannel dress.

"There's a town nearby," Carrick said as the woman sat them down to a meal of fried eggs, ham, and cornbread, "but durned if I can ever remember the name of it."

"Cleveland," the woman prompted. She was eyeing the handsome Carrick with more than passing interest, Amelia thought.

"Cleveland! That's it. Just like that Yankee town up north. It was right on the tip of my tongue and I couldn't spit it out."

"It's not far from here," she continued. "But, if you've got your directions all mixed up, I can help you."

She disappeared into the bedroom for a minute and returned, carrying an atlas. "My son used this in school, year before last," she said, carefully tearing out a full-page map and placing it on the table. "It shows all of eastern Tennessee and some of North Carolina. We're right here, and there's Cleveland, just a few miles east."

"Where's your son?" Amelia asked when she noticed their buxom hostess leaning against Carrick's shoulder as she pointed to the map.

"Down in the village at school. I'm gonna make sure that boy gets a good education so he doesn't have to work with his hands all his life."

"Your husband at work?" Amelia asked casually.

"Killed in the war six months ago," she answered with no outward sign of emotion, although her hazel eyes showed a flicker of pain as she reached for the coffee pot on the cook stove. She refilled their cups with a brew that tasted like it was concocted from rye grain. Evidently the blockade of foreign imports was working.

The way they stuffed the food down after their long fast must have convinced the woman they had told the truth about being hungry, even if she wondered about their story of being lost.

When they finished, Carrick paid the woman, thanked her for the food and map, and they quickly departed.

Amelia marveled again at how much the food picked up her strength and her spirits as they set out toward Cleveland. At least now they had a better idea of where they were going. When she'd concocted the plot of stealing the gold and silver shipment and delivering it to the Yankees, she certainly had never dreamed events would take this turn —

the bulk of the precious metal in the bottom of the Oostanaula River, and she and her son and the rest of the raiders scattered in the mountains on foot as refugees from angry Rebels. Ah, well, one took chances, then waited to see what suffering and triumph fate had in store.

They continued to descend the mountain and walked across the wide valley floor. Toward evening their appetites returned, awakened by the food they'd eaten a few hours before. Emboldened by their earlier success, they selected an isolated log house and knocked. At first no one seemed to be at home. But, just as they were leaving, the door was opened by a tall woman of about fifty, wearing a floor-length blue dress. Her dark hair, streaked with silver, was carefully coifed. But nothing could soften the effect of the long, lean face that gave her a severe appearance.

"Come in and rest yourselves," the lady said, swinging open the door and eyeing first their dirty, trail-worn clothing, and then giving Amelia a curious glance.

For some reason, as they stepped inside, Amelia thought of the story of Hansel and Gretel and the wicked witch.

The woman introduced herself as Lucille Gruber, and the refugees gave the same false names they'd used before.

Very shortly they were seated at a table with a blue checked cloth, forking up pancakes and blackstrap molasses with sausage patties.

"Are you traveling?" Lucille Gruber asked.

"We're on our way to Harrison," Carrick answered promptly. They had rehearsed their story and selected the nearby village of Harrison as their fictitious destination.

As Mrs. Gruber went about fixing a pitcher of cider, Amelia noticed that she was giving them a close scrutiny at every opportunity. Amelia had seen that look before and could almost read the woman's mind — Mrs. Gruber was not satisfied with their story and was trying to decide just what to do about it. The men continued to eat, apparently unaware of the sharp looks she gave them. Amelia was becoming uneasy. She sipped at a glass of cider to moisten her dry throat.

Finally Lucille Gruber turned from the stove and faced them. "You are Union men!" she declared.

They looked up, startled.

"Oh, don't try to deny it," she hurried on when Amelia opened her mouth to object. "There are a lot of Union people in this region. You're trying to escape the Confederate conscript. I know Union men when I see them."

"We were in the Confederate Army," Carrick lied. "We got separated from our unit and are trying to make our way home." He looked at Amelia. "We ran across this lady on the road a few miles from here. She's from Harrison and volunteered to guide us that far."

"No, no. You're Union. You have that look about you. Even your accent gives you away." She looked at Amelia. "I'm not sure how you fit into this, but somehow you're helping them escape the Rebs. I know a goodly number of people in the village of Harrison, and I've never heard your names or seen any of you around here before."

The men were armed, and Amelia expected Carrick and her son to pull their pistols and cover their getaway. She edged her chair back and thought of scooping up some of the cooked sausage patties to take with them.

Just then the door opened and a tall, robust man walked in.

"Peter, these are Union people," Lucy greeted him.

Amelia half rose from the table, convinced they would have to fight their way out. Carrick and Josiah were on their feet.

"Good!" Peter boomed in a hearty voice. "We're Union, too," he said. "And we'll do anything to help you."

Amelia and her son looked at each other, then at Carrick for leadership. Was this some kind of trick to trap them into admitting they were Union, then have them arrested?

"She's mistaken us for someone else," Carrick said calmly, although Amelia noticed his knuckles whiten where he was gripping the back of his chair. She saw that Peter Gruber had a pistol thrust through his broad belt, although his manner belied any hostile intent.

"They're not admitting to it," Lucille Gruber continued. "But they're Union through and through. You can bet on it."

Amelia wondered what had given them away, or was this just a bluff to get them to admit their loyalty?

Peter Gruber looked at them with calm assurance. "You can say or not say what you wish. My wife is almost never mistaken about matters like this. It's an instinct with her. We've lived too long among these Southern Rebels not to know the difference."

"Believe what you wish," Amelia added, trying her best to look bewildered.

"Peter, sit down and let's finish supper. Then we'll do what we can to help these good folks on their way."

Amelia found that, in spite of this surprise and uncertainty, she had not lost her appetite, and ate her fill for the first time in several days.

"Old Major Snow's cavalry is patrolling the area," Lucy said as they finished the meal. "Peter can probably tell you where they're likely to be so you can avoid them."

"Who's Major Snow?" Josiah asked.

"A man from Cleveland who raised and outfitted a company of volunteers and gave himself the rank of major,"

Peter laughed. "But" — he jabbed his fork at them from across the table — "don't take him lightly. He's not about to confront any armed men in battle. He's appointed himself the task of heading off and rounding up Union sympathizers on the move who're trying to avoid conscription into the Confederate Army. A worthy cause, but not too dangerous for armed cavalry."

"We have a good place to hide you until we can slip you on north," Lucy said, eyeing them.

Amelia was suddenly conscious of her own bedraggled appearance.

"And I have some clothes you can have," Lucille added, looking at Amelia. "Those boots are coming apart. And I'm sure they're heavy."

"Thank you," Amelia nodded.

The three refugees never actually admitted their true loyalties, but the Grubers apparently took silence for assent. After dark, Peter guided them outside, across a back pasture and through a patch of woods to a vacant, run-down little house.

"This is where Lucy and I lived when we first bought this property, long before we built our present house," he said.

Amelia thought it looked dreary and forlorn in the light of the rising moon.

Gruber led them inside, and lighted a lantern he carried. A two-room place, devoid of furniture, but at least it had a wooden floor.

"We still use this root cellar," Gruber said, scuffing away straw from a trap door in the plank floor, and lifting it by an iron ring. A musty smell rose from the darkness, and Amelia automatically brushed her hands over the clean, cotton shirt and pants cut off at the ankles that Lucy had provided.

" 'Tain't much, but you'll be safe here for now. There're air holes enough in the floor that you'll be fine." He held the lantern high for them to see the wooden steps down into the seven-foot-deep cellar. Carrick led the way, followed by Josiah who turned to hand his mother down last. "Get you some sleep and I'll be back in a few hours with some vittles," Gruber said, letting down the trap door over their heads.

His boots scuffed straw back over the trap door. Then the sound of footsteps receded and silence fell.

Before the lantern was withdrawn, Amelia saw that the cellar was very small — barely room enough for the three of them to lie down, side-by-side, on the dirt floor.

"At least it's dry, and warm," she said, mostly to hear her own voice in the utter blackness. She could only feel the men shifting about close by.

"I feel a little claustrophobic," Carrick said. "Think I'll roll up my jacket and prop up that trap door just a little. Get some more air, too. We can shut it when daylight comes."

"I'm exhausted," Amelia said, sitting down on a board that formed a low shelf against the dirt wall, and pulling off her shoes. They were flat-heeled women's work shoes, but they fit reasonably well, and she was especially grateful for the clean, dry men's socks. She had managed to conceal the piece of a gold bar in her jacket pocket when she'd changed into the clean clothes. So far, so good. As she lay down to sleep, she said a silent prayer of thanks for the Grubers and people like them. If they were ever to escape to safety, it would be with help like this.

The next thing Amelia knew, she awoke to sprinkles of dirt falling on her face and head. It was daylight and

Carrick had climbed the steps to lay the trap door back on the floor above. She heard voices, then saw Peter Gruber hand him a small basket. "Look underneath," he said.

Carrick lifted out several dried ears of corn and handed the basket down for Amelia to see — fresh-baked biscuits and fried bacon, wrapped in a white napkin. Plenty for three. Her stomach grumbled.

"Rest here the remainder of the day," Gruber said. "If everything is clear, I'll come and get you just before dark, and point the way north toward the river."

Amelia enjoyed her day of rest almost as much as the food that restored her strength. She had no salve for her blistered feet, but the dry socks and the comfortable, light shoes were a blessing. Even if she had to walk another thirty miles, she felt she had the stamina now, if they could take it in easy stages. She would let Carrick make the decisions about where and when to go and how to talk their way out of trouble. He had certainly proven capable enough so far.

True to his word, Gruber again showed up at dusk with cornbread and fried ham. They all ate and had a good drink of cold water from a nearby spring.

"Cut straight through these woods for a quarter mile and you'll come to a road. Turn left on the road and follow it until you come to Harrison. You can by-pass the village." He proceeded to tell them how.

Carrick nodded. "We've got a map of the area. We can make it on north to the Tennessee River from there."

"Good luck to you," Gruber said enthusiastically, gripping a hand of each of them in turn. "Lucy said to tell you to go with God."

"Thanks for your help. We couldn't have made it without you," Josiah said.

"Keep a sharp look-out and avoid any strangers,"

Gruber said. "You're not safe yet."

The three of them waved good bye and faded into the forest.

They walked for hours, and Amelia felt more comfortable than she had since they'd abandoned the train. For one thing, the food and rest had restored her energy. The shoes and the clean clothing were a great comfort, and they were walking on a road that was relatively level and free of mud.

Sometime late in the night, they came to the outskirts of a village they took to be Harrison and made the wide detour outlined by Gruber, climbing over rail fences and crossing farmers' fields in the waning moonlight. Luckily no dogs barked, and they had the cover of thick stands of timber part of the way.

Safely around the village, they emerged onto the road and stopped for a short breather. A grayness was stealing up from the eastern sky and pushing back the dark. An early-rising cardinal began a tentative whistling in the nearby woods. Then a mockingbird joined in as nature sensed the coming day.

Carrick took advantage of the dim light to study his map. "Looks like the quickest way is to angle off just a bit to the east of here," he said, then folded the map, and shoved it into his coat pocket. "Right now the best thing we can do is find some deep cover and get a few hours' sleep."

As they turned, the rumble of hoofs sounded from somewhere close.

"Quick!" Carrick called, grabbing Amelia's arm and running for the woods several yards away.

But it was too late. Before they'd taken five steps, twenty armed horsemen trotted into view from around a bend and reined up in a semicircle, cutting off any escape. Josiah lifted his hand slowly from his holstered pistol as the three of them drew back against each other.

"Well, what have we here?" a man in front exclaimed, keeping a tight rein on his excited mount that was jumping and turning.

"Out kinda early, aren't you folks?" he said, giving them a hard look. "Or maybe you've been up all night."

In the uncertain light, Amelia saw a tall, rangy man who wore a felt hat with an ostrich plume arching back over the broad brim.

"I'm Major Snow and this is my company." He glanced over his shoulder at his lieutenant. "Have the men stand down and be easy for a spell. We need to ask these early hikers a few questions."

Amelia felt her heart sink, hoping Carrick's powers of persuasion were up to the challenge.

Chapter Seventeen
deflated

Major Snow handed the reins of his mount to a lieutenant, then stood with his feet wide apart and hands on hips, regarding the trio. The wide, plumed hat, the sweeping mustache, the scarlet sash, the saber with the tarnished gold braid swinging at his hip, his arrogant stance — all made Amelia think of a drawing she'd once seen in a history book of a musketeer during the French Revolution. Apparently it was just the impression he was hoping to create, when he said: "I'm not in the habit of taking prisoners. Anyone who falls into my hands is usually left swinging by his neck from a tree."

The trio remained silent, but Amelia had to bite her cheeks to keep from bursting into laughter. She had seen her boys utter just such nonsense with as much dramatic flair when they used to play at being pirates.

Apparently thinking they were duly impressed, he continued, asking their names and where they were from.

Carrick answered for all of them, giving different false names and saying they were on their way to Harrison. He repeated the story that they were separated from their regiment, became lost in the woods, and Amelia had offered to guide them as far as Harrison.

"Amelia Dunn?" Snow repeated, cocking his head. "I know most of the families in Harrison, but no one named Dunn."

"That was my husband's name," Amelia said. "He was from Atlanta."

"What's your maiden name?"

Amelia was caught, but never twitched as she replied with the first surname that popped into her head. "Johnson." It was common enough. Maybe her bluff would work.

Snow paused, apparently trying to recall the Johnsons. "Old Abner Johnson's daughter?"

"The same," she answered.

"Liar!" he snapped. "Abner Johnson was a crazy old bachelor who died eight years ago. Never had no kids who carried his name." He eyed their dirty, ragged clothes. "You jaspers are out of uniform. In fact, I got me a strong hunch you ain't soldiers a-tall. You're running away from Confederate conscription. You ought to be shot as traitors for wanting to join the damned Yankees. . . ."

"We ain't got the slightest intention of joining up with the Yankees!" Carrick interrupted a little hotly. "Those damned blue bellies are fast ruining the South and its people."

Snow paced from side to side, one hand on his saber hilt, the other stroking his mustache as he regarded them out of the corners of his eyes. Posturing for his men, Amelia thought, while he tried to decide what to do with them.

He turned to the lieutenant who was holding his horse. "Search them! Maybe they got some identification on them." Amelia thought, he probably never did anything himself, except talk.

"You know common soldiers don't carry anything on

them, but maybe their own billfolds," Carrick said mildly, with a shrug. "And we've done lost ours."

"Huh!" Snow snorted. "For all I know, you may belong to those spies and bridge burners!"

Amelia cringed at the accidental accuracy of this statement. She dared not look at Carrick or her son.

The short, chunky lieutenant grunted as he dismounted. The growing daylight revealed the food stains on his yellow silk sash as he approached. He seemed to take great delight in running his hands up and down Amelia's body and slipping his hands into her pockets. She held her breath. It was too late to hide the gold.

"Oh, ho! Lookee here!" He held up the square lump of yellow metal.

Surprised comments and low whistles rippled through the company. Those in the rear tried to push their horses forward to see.

"Check the others!" Snow's face was set in a grim mask as he held out a hand for the gold.

The fat lieutenant removed the pistols from the holsters of both men, then held up the other half of the gold bar retrieved from Josiah's coat pocket.

"Gawd," one of the nearest men breathed. "Lemme touch it. I ain't never seen nothing like that. Is it real?" He put out his hand, but Snow slapped it aside and took the partial ingot.

"You're damn' right it's real," he said, hefting a chunk of the precious metal in each hand. The gold seemed to glow a dull yellow in the pre-sunrise light. "And I think I know where these came from." He paused for dramatic effect, examining the markings stamped into the soft metal.

During several seconds of silence, the only sounds they heard were the twittering of birds in the nearby trees, the shifting of the horses, the squeak of leather.

"This is a part of the gold and silver shipment from the Dahlonega mint," he declared, staring at Amelia. "I saw a story in yesterday's *Chattanooga Gazette* about it. A woman slickered the guards and stole the whole damn' wagonload. Then, somehow, she got it on the train with those bridge burners." He paused. "And this, boys, is the woman!"

Amelia quailed inwardly at the stares of the men who regarded her with renewed curiosity — or was it respect?

"You sure they're disarmed . . . no hide-out guns or knives?" Snow asked as he stuffed the two chunks of gold into his saddlebags.

"They're clean," the lieutenant replied.

"I'm placing you under arrest," Snow said, turning toward them. "We'll round up three horses and take you to Chattanooga and turn you over to the authorities," he said, reverting to a formal, legal tone.

Amelia turned her gaze to Josiah and Carrick. She could hardly keep the tears back. After all they'd been through, they'd been surprised and captured without a struggle.

In mid-afternoon, the trio, escorted by Major Snow and a squad of picked men, drew rein at a two-story jail in Chattanooga. The square, brick building had a pitched roof, but had been built on the side of a hill so that the upper floor approached ground level on the high side of the slope.

First they had been brought to the headquarters of General Ledbetter who had questioned them at length, and individually. Satisfied that these were, indeed, three of the train thieves, he confiscated the two halves of the gold bar as evidence, then gave Major Snow and his men the honor of delivering the captives to jail to await trial.

The prisoners were not allowed to converse among

themselves at any time, but there was nothing Amelia wanted to say that she cared to have overheard. So the three were left alone with their own thoughts.

"The Swims Jail," Snow said with some surprise, as he dismounted inside the walled yard. "This used to be a lockup for captured runaway slaves. Guess they ran out of jail space."

"Old Hark Swims is raking in some cash if the gov'ment is paying him so much a head for all his Federal prisoners," one of the men said, as he pushed Amelia and the two men through a door into the upper floor of the jail. Snow stepped up to each of the captives with a Bowie knife and sawed through the cord that bound their hands in front of them.

With a great sense of relief, Amelia rubbed her chafed and swollen hands and wrists, then flexed her arms that had been held in nearly the same position during the long ride.

"Got three more for ya, Hark," Major Snow said. "Take good care of them. They're part of that train-thieving bunch. The old lady, here, even stole some gold from the mint."

Without replying, a white-haired man with narrow eyes and tobacco-stained teeth went behind his desk, dipped a pen into an inkwell, and entered their false names into a large book. Then he took two sets of manacles from a hook on the wall and handcuffed the men's hands in front of them.

Amelia wondered if she was going to be housed with any male prisoners. The back half of this upper floor apparently contained cells. Beyond an open door into a dim hallway she could sense some figures stirring.

As if in answer to her silent question, old Hark Swims put his pen back in its holder, got up, and pulled a ring of keys from a drawer. "Got just the place," he said, selecting a large key. "Right here where I can eyeball her."

He unlocked the door of a cage that was about nine by twelve feet. "Just shipped off a half dozen prisoners to Virginia."

She stepped into the iron cage that took up most of the room. It was formed of metal slats, crossing each other at right angles about six inches apart, forming a grid. The roof was of the same material, about two feet below the ceiling of the room. The floor was wooden planks.

The iron door clanged shut behind her, sending a chill up her spine. She turned, and looked out through the grill at her son and Carrick who were being taken to the other side of the room where their hats and coats were removed.

In all her fifty-two years, Amelia had never been incarcerated. It gave her a feeling she could not describe — an eeriness almost bordering on panic at the loss of freedom, a feeling of vulnerability she'd never known before. Yet, in a way, she felt detached, as if observing this happening to someone else, watching the inevitable. She was only acting out her rôle in a play that had been scripted by the Almighty long ago.

She looked around. At least the cage was big and light and airy. She would just settle down to wait and see what developed.

Carrick glanced at Amelia Waymier's cage. He should have known the Rebs would find a separate place for her. It was unthinkable that she would be incarcerated with any of the men. He and Josiah would most likely be put into one of the cells down the hallway.

He tried to read the face of their jailer, but failed. Swims was an old man of about sixty with a withered face, leathery skin, and an abundance of white hair. Having lived a long time and seen his share of suffering, perhaps the old man would show compassion to his prisoners.

"What do you want me to do with them?" Swims asked in a whiny voice.

"General Ledbetter said to put 'em in the hole," one of the guards replied.

Swims went to the middle of the room, knelt down, and inserted a large key into a hole in the floor and gave it a turn. Then, with an effort that seemed almost beyond the strength of the lean old man, he heaved up a ponderous trap door about four feet square and let it crash backward onto the floor. A rush of hot air with a sickening stench rose from the depths of the black opening.

Carrick recoiled instinctively, but the bayonets of the guards pricked his back and he stopped. He dared not look at Josiah.

Swims dragged a ladder from where it lay along the wall. "Stand from under!" he cried, thrusting one end down the hole.

Along with the fetid air, a murmur of voices rose from the depths.

"What about these?" Carrick asked, holding up his cuffed hands.

"Wear 'em!" the guard snapped. "They look good on you," he added with a malicious grin.

"Down you go!" Another guard nudged him with the point of his bayonet.

Swims held a lighted candle aloft that did nothing to penetrate the darkness below.

Holding his breath and feeling for the unseen rungs, Carrick led the way down, foot by foot, until the suffocating blackness swallowed him. He stepped off at the bottom onto a yielding body. Someone cursed and rolled out from under his foot, nearly tripping him. Carrick wedged himself against sweating, stinking, unseen bodies of living men to clear a space for Josiah who was right behind him.

Then the ladder was slowly drawn up, and the trap door fell with a *thud,* shutting out all light and much of the air.

"Josiah?" In a moment of sudden panic, he reached for Waymier in the darkness. A hand on his friend's arm gave some reassurance of his own sanity. The blackness, the heat, and the stench made him feel as if he were smothering. Perspiration began oozing from every pore, and he fought down a sudden urge to vomit.

"You all right?" came Josiah's calm voice.

Carrick relaxed his fierce grip on the young man's arm. "Yeah." He swallowed. "I'll be OK in a minute." He tried to breathe shallowly, forcing himself to get a grip on his emotions by diverting his thoughts to something else. It took a supreme act of will. All that came to mind was the black hole of Calcutta where a group of Englishmen had died in just such a pit in India a century before. He thrust this thought aside and visualized himself in a sunny field above ground with trees bending to a fresh wind. His panic gradually subsided. "Stay close," he said to Josiah, as he wiped the clammy sweat from his forehead.

Within a couple of minutes his eyes grew accustomed to the darkness. Instead of being totally blind, he could now see a little of the afternoon light filtering through the barred windows near the top of the twelve-foot room. They'd entered the jail by an outside stairway on the high side of the brick structure. The windows he now saw were apparently near ground level on the opposite wall.

The other men in the room had not spoken, but Carrick could sense them shifting around in the crowded space.

Bearded, ragged, filthy, hollow-eyed men regarded them with a silent, spectral interest. He shivered in spite of the heat.

The throng parted for them as he and Josiah approached one wall, and felt their way around the room. He discovered it was thirteen feet square and found another barred window eighteen inches tall at head height beneath the outside stairway. Pushing his face close to it, he was able to suck in enough fresh air to revive himself, at least partially. By the dim light from this window, Carrick counted eighteen other prisoners crammed into the hole. The men's clothing was in tatters. The only furnishings in the room were four buckets for water and slops. The sole access was by way of the overhead trap door. The frequent coughing and stench of excreta told him how sick these men had become.

"God, what a place," Carrick murmured in horror.

"We'll make it," Josiah said. "Don't worry." His voice was far from reassuring. "Just stay calm. These men have been here for some time, and they're still surviving."

"It's tough at first, but you get used to it," a voice said at Carrick's elbow. "I'm John Wolford from Knoxville," he added. "Who might you boys be?"

Carrick introduced the two of them.

"You wouldn't be part of the train thieves, would you?"

"We are."

"Well, by damn! It's great to meet you!" Wolford wrung each of their hands in turn. "We heard rumors about that, even down here. Mighty brave thing, I say."

"We failed," Carrick said simply.

"Maybe so, maybe not. You sure charged us with a lot of hope. And I'd wager you did the same for a bunch of others. The Rebs know they're not safe anywhere now."

The men in the crowded space listened and added their own comments.

"C'mon, tell us about it. Give us the details," Wolford urged.

Apparently they were celebrities to these poor wretches, Carrick thought as he stood next to the tiny window for what little light and air it provided. He gave a thumbnail sketch of their adventure. With Josiah adding details here and there, Carrick unfolded their story for the next hour, pausing only to answer questions from the dimly seen crowd around them. He omitted the part about Amelia Waymier and the gold bullion.

When he finished, the afternoon light had grown dim. He couldn't remember the last time he'd talked so much, and he was worn out. The men shuffled away, talking quietly among themselves. Carrick, his hands manacled in front of him by a short length of chain, sat down awkwardly on the floor. He and Josiah leaned their backs against the wall. As the newcomers, they were given extra space and the privilege of sitting near the only source of light and air. Carrick suspected the fetid atmosphere and lack of oxygen might be causing the fatigue he felt. Or maybe it was the mental let-down from losing his freedom.

As he slumped against the wall, his eye distinguished among the grimy faces the presence of a Negro in the room. The black man caught and held Carrick's gaze, then edged forward, his round mahogany face shining with perspiration in the dim light.

"My name's Alex," he said, dropping to one knee to be on a level with the seated men. Carrick was not surprised that he made no offer to shake hands. "I'm a free man, but dey's had me in dis here jail for a few months now."

"If you're free, why are you locked up?" Josiah asked.

"Dis used to be called Swims's Nigra jail befoe da war, 'cause dey used it for runaways when they catched 'em," Alex replied, apparently thinking they needed to know this history before he answered the question. "I was workin' fo' wages and coming in to Chattanooga on an errand when a patrol snatched me up. I didn't have no papers showin' I was free, so they clapped me in here."

"Didn't you tell them who you were working for?"

"Mos' certainly. But dey claims dey ain't no such person. Fact is, dis happens all da time 'round here." He lowered his head and picked at a bug on the packed dirt and sand floor. "Dey figures I's a runaway and flogs me regular to make me say it. Dey'll hold me till my master comes. When he don't come after a few months, da jailer's free to sell me at auction and keep da money to pay expenses o' my keep."

"What expenses?" Josiah snorted.

Carrick was outraged by this tale, but Alex seemed to take everything matter-of-factly.

After a few more exchanges, the men lapsed into silence. The oppressiveness of the place weighed down on everyone's spirits. After the excitement and novelty of two newcomers and their tale of adventure, the men sank into their former torpor.

The light from the tiny windows gradually faded, and no food or water was forthcoming. Two hours after dark, the men, with a shifting and muttering, prepared for sleep. Apparently they'd worked out a system, since there was not enough room for everyone to lie down where he pleased.

"Let me show you how this is done," Wolford said as the men began to find their places on the floor. He pointed out where the buckets were placed in two corners, to be out of the way in case someone wanted to use the latrine at night.

Then the men lay down in two rows, like cupped spoons, each row of heads to opposite walls. Since no more than nine could fit in each row, Carrick and Waymier were assigned to lie end to end between the two rows of feet. Some of the prisoners' ankles were chained together; others had their hands manacled with short chains.

Carrick discovered during the long, restless night that if one man turned over in his sleep, the others had to turn as well. The endless hours he lay awake were filled with groanings and mutterings of the prisoners in their sleep, punctuated by the clanking and rattling of chains.

When Carrick opened his bleary eyes to the dim light of morning, he realized that he was no longer aware of the stench of the place. Such, he reflected, is the adaptability of the human animal.

As the men began to stir and sit up, there was a chorus of coughing and hacking and the men spat into the latrine buckets. Given the circumstances these men had endured for weeks and months, Carrick wondered if some of them might have contracted consumption.

Carrick was remarking about this to Wolford in the semi-darkness when they heard the tramping of many feet on the wooden stairway outside the wall, along with the clanking of chains. Then the thumping steps were overhead, and the trap door was thrown back. A rush of cool, fresh air flooded down on them. Every man leaned toward the air as a thirsty horde for water. "Lord, Lord, if only they'd leave the trap door open!" Wolford moaned.

The ladder was thrust down the hole, and three men began to descend, one after another.

"Oh, please don't put any more down here!" Wolford cried. "We can't stand it. We'll die."

The plea was ignored. As soon as the last man had

cleared the bottom rung, the ladder was yanked up, and the trap door slammed, shutting off the flow of fresh air.

In the dim light, Carrick took a closer look at the newcomers, and his heart sank. "Oh, no! Andrews, Knight, and Ross!"

Chapter Eighteen
horrors of the hole

"Mister Andrews!" Carrick cried, turning the big man toward him. "We were hoping you'd gotten away."

"Carrick, is that you?" the bearded leader said, fumbling to grip his hand. "I can hardly see."

"You'll get used to it, sir."

"Josiah Waymier. You're here, too."

J. J. Andrews looked worn and ragged, splattered with mud. Apparently he'd had a hard time of it. "Sorry, boys. It just wasn't meant to be, I guess. But we'll figure out something. We're not done yet."

As shocked as he was to see his leader and two more of the raiders, Carrick still felt a sense of relief that he and Waymier at least had some company of their own.

"This is a hard place," Josiah said, shaking hands with Knight and Ross.

"Sergeant-Major Ross, I'm glad to see you're alive," Carrick said. "What happened in the tunnel?"

Ross shook his head sadly. "We've got some stories to swap."

"I just saw Amelia in a cage upstairs," Andrews said.

"Was she all right?" Josiah asked. "How're they treating her?"

"She looked fine," Andrews said, "but I hardly had a chance to give her a quick nod before they shoved us down here."

"Looks like you boys have a lot to catch up on," Wolford said. "Come over by the window where you can talk a little easier." The rest of the East Tennesseans parted and let Carrick and Waymier accompany the three newcomers to the far wall where the outside light was beginning to strengthen and a whisper of fresh morning air was seeping through the bars.

"What a hole!" Knight said, grimacing at the foul atmosphere.

Ross told his tale first, detailing how his attempt to derail the *General* had failed. He'd tried to make his way north on foot, by night, following the railway, then had stolen a horse from a farm and ridden bareback. But not far from Ringgold he'd run into a patrol of citizens who were scouring the countryside for the train thieves. He'd tried to ride off, but they'd shot his horse from under him. He'd come up, firing his pistol, and had wounded two of his pursuers, but had been surrounded with no shelter and was forced to surrender or die. Even though he didn't say so, a swollen eye and lip testified to the hard usage he'd suffered at the hands of his captors.

Andrews and Knight had been run to earth by bloodhounds. They were sleeping on an island in the Tennessee River when two boatloads of manhunters surprised them. They lost the men in the thick timber, who then quickly sent one of their number for some bloodhounds. Andrews and Knight had no boat and so were waiting for darkness. They threw the dogs off the scent by wading along shore in the shallow water and then climbed a tree. As luck would have it, one of the men, searching the lower end of the island, happened to look up and spot the two men in the leafy branches. Knight fired at him, and the two men jumped down and made a run for it. Andrews's powder was wet, but Knight wounded two of the dogs and one of the manhunters before they were cornered at the end of the island and captured. Angered by the shooting of their dogs, two of the Rebels had started to whip Knight with a tree branch until Andrews placated them by promising to come along peacefully if they would desist.

While the raiders were exchanging stories, the trap door was opened once more and Swims's white head appeared.

"Here's your breakfast, boys!" He lowered a bucket on a rope to eager, waiting hands.

A bond had sprung up among the East Tennesseans because the food was divided with scrupulous attention to fairness, each receiving the same amount, even to the weakest who could barely stand, and Alex, the Negro. This sharing extended to the five new arrivals. As Carrick ate his portion, consisting of a tiny piece of cornbread and a sliver of old pork, he knew it wasn't a fourth of what he needed or wanted.

"We get fed twice a day," Wolford said, noticing Carrick licking his greasy fingers. "But don't worry. After you're here a few months, you won't be near as hungry."

Carrick nodded, but silently resolved to try any means of escape rather than stay here that long. He could easily see how the strength of these gaunt, bearded men had been eroded over time. He had already noted that their matted hair and rags of clothing were infested with parasitic fleas and lice. Their skin was layered with accumulated grime from lack of water for washing, their bodies debilitated by lack of exercise and fresh air. Somehow, some way he would not let that happen to himself and the other raiders.

"There were a few rats down here when we first came," Wolford said. "They were such a nuisance, we didn't put up with them long."

"Killed 'em off?"

He nodded. "And ate 'em."

Carrick had to swallow twice to subdue a sudden urge to retch up what little food he'd just eaten. He turned away to get a whiff of fresh air near the only accessible window. No one was allowed to stand in front of the window and block the air for more than a few minutes at a time.

"God, these poor devils have been reduced to eating raw rat," Josiah whispered as he joined Carrick. "I'm surprised they're not all dead."

"Won't be long before we're in the same pathetic shape if we don't figure a way out of here," Carrick said. "And we'll have to do it before our strength gives out." Privately he wondered if most of the other men were not more than thirty or forty years old. In his experience, men in their teens and twenties needed much more food just to maintain their vitality. Older people could get by on relatively little, and thus had a greater capacity for endurance. But when he looked around at the dull, haggard faces in the dungeon, it dawned on him that maybe these men only *looked* a lot older.

"Have you got any money left?" Carrick asked quietly.

"A few coins. Maybe a dollar," Josiah said. "After they found that hunk of gold on me, they weren't much interested in a little change."

"I've got a five dollar note hid in my boot," Carrick said. "Let's check with Andrews. If he and Knight and Ross have any, maybe we can buy some food for these fellas."

The other three raiders had a total of $4.76. The next

time the trap door was opened to haul up their latrine buckets, Carrick called up in his most civil tone: "Mister Swims, could we buy some extra food?"

"Depends," the old man answered. "Got any money?"

"Some."

"Lemme see it."

Carrick made a show of producing five dollars and some change — about half of their total.

The old jailer seemed to mellow at the sight. "What do you want for it?"

The starving men were talking together behind Carrick until Wolford spoke up. "The boys said the money would go further if we buy some wheat bread and molasses, since that's pretty cheap."

"All right." Swims's head disappeared. In a few seconds he was back and lowered a clean bucket. "Put it in there."

He hauled it up, returned their empty slop bucket, and slammed the trap door.

"Thanks, boys. We won't forget you for this," Wolford told the raiders.

Late that afternoon, the trap door opened and Swims lowered their bucket containing the usual sparse cornbread and aging strips of meat.

"Where's our bread and molasses?" Carrick yelled up after the bucket was emptied.

"Oh, sorry, but I lost that money," Swims said, pulling on the bucket rope.

"Officer of the Guard!" Carrick shouted at the top of his voice.

"I'll send him right along." Swims grinned amiably, showing tobacco-stained teeth.

Carrick sucked in great lungs full of fresh air, grateful for the two minutes it took the military man to arrive from the stockade outside.

"What's the problem?" he called down.

Carrick related what had happened.

"Anybody who'd trust that old reprobate with money deserves what he gets," the officer said. The trap door slammed them into semi-darkness, cutting off the cackling of Swims's laughter in the background.

At that moment, Carrick hated enough to kill. His hands flexed involuntarily as he pictured his fingers gripping Swims's turkey neck, choking the life out of the thieving jailer. At the same time he was embarrassed for having dashed the hopes of the men around him. What a fool he was for trusting the man! But it had been their only hope. At least, they hadn't squandered *all* of their funds.

"Don't worry about it," Andrews consoled him. "Not your fault. We had to try."

"I sure had my mouth fixed for molasses and wheat bread," one of the men muttered.

"Ah been thinkin' 'bout sweet potatoes and ham," Alex said cheerfully. "Reckon I'll just keep on doing that. Can't get no worse."

"Yeah," Wolford said. "What've we got to be in a funk about, boys? At least they aren't draggin' us out every few days to give us a lashing, like they do poor Alex, here."

A murmur of agreement flowed through the crowded room.

"Hell, we've made it this far. We'll make it the rest of the way!"

A ragged cheer went up, and the men seemed to relax into a better mood.

Carrick had to admire their courage, knowing they had little hope of escape, except by way of death, or the remote possibility of prisoner exchange.

* * * * *

The three new raiders had been in the hole only five days when an armed guard came and called Andrews out one morning.

He returned later that afternoon.

"They put me on trial," he reported to their eager questions when the trap door had slammed above. "Couldn't call it a court-martial since I'm a civilian."

"Did they give you a chance to talk?" Ross asked.

"Yes. I couldn't deny what I did. Too many people saw me. I tried to claim the Federals would allow me to sell goods and trade across Southern lines if I would just steal a train for the Union Army. As a blockade-runner furnishing scarce items, I would benefit the South as well as myself. But that story didn't hold up. They knew our mission was to destroy bridges, since they saw the burning boxcars. They pressured me to name our engineer, but I refused."

"Thanks for that," Knight said.

Andrews nodded. "For some reason, they blame the engineer, even though you were just following orders." He paused thoughtfully. "Boys, it's going to go hard with me. But I think you'll be all right if you stick to this story . . . tell them you are only soldiers following orders and had no idea of your mission until you got to Georgia. Don't let them know you were volunteers who were briefed beforehand."

They discussed this and rehearsed their story until each man knew the details by heart. If they were separated and questioned, there would be no inconsistencies.

In spite of their determination to find a way out, all the raiders together could not come up with an escape plan that sounded remotely feasible. The window well showed the thickness of the wall to be three layers of brick. The East

Tennesseans had long ago given up attempts to chip out the mortar to loosen them, and the sandy soil of the floor had defeated all efforts at tunneling. One man, standing on another's shoulders, could reach the plank ceiling, but they had to stand close to the wall for balance. One man had a Case knife, but it was practically useless against the heavy wood.

Gambling games were devised, using pieces of straw. Stories of their former lives were told and retold. Each man had his own guess as to how the war was going — anything to fill the time and take their minds off their misery. The floor and their bodies were covered with lice. Adding to the torment, the iron shackles constantly chafed raw sores on their wrists and ankles. As the days grew warmer, they were nearly always thirsty, perspiring in the heat and stifling atmosphere. Swims refused to fill the water buckets as often as needed.

Rumor had it that old Swims was charging a fee for visitors to view the prisoners — money he used to buy rum, his favorite drink. The old jailer, even though drunk much of the time, was always careful never to lower the ladder unless armed guards were present. Nearly every time he opened the trap to lower their cornbread and maggot-filled bacon, Carrick saw several curious faces staring down at them.

"Old Abe's abolition dogs don't look so tough now, do they?" one of the visitors scoffed.

"Come down here and I'll show you who's tough, you monkey-faced Reb!" one of the prisoners shot back.

This jawing went on every time the trap was opened and the prisoners vied to come up with the most inventive, insulting names and curses to rile the visitors. Sometimes Swims had to drop the door quickly to prevent some red-faced hothead from jumping down the hole and mixing it up with the prisoners.

"About the only entertainment we get," Wolford commented to Carrick and several of the raiders about two weeks after Andrews's arrival.

"I encourage it all I can. Frustrating as it is to cuss at those Reb roosters, at least it keeps the boys' fighting spirit alive."

They eventually entrusted their remaining five dollars to the officer of the guard to buy them some additional food. He brought some bread and decent ham. It was wholesome and tasty. However, when it was divided equally, it barely furnished each man enough to equal one of his daily rations.

To help fill the long tedious hours in the hole, Carrick, Waymier, Andrews, Knight, and Ross held endless discussions about the possibilities of being exchanged for Rebel prisoners held by the North. Ross and Knight seemed more hopeful than the others. But, since they were cut off from any news of the war, it was all mere speculation. Rumor abounded, however. Carrick, Waymier, and Andrews put no faith in the exchange program.

Three days after Andrew's trial, the men were sitting next to the wall, discussing some means of escape. They heard a stirring above, and the trap door opened.

"It ain't meal time," Wolford said.

"I'll take the fresh air any time," Waymier said, scratching at the vermin under his shirt.

The ladder was lowered and a uniformed officer descended, covered by the muskets of two guards above.

"J. J. Andrews?" he said, looking around in the gloom.

Andrews rose, and stepped forward. The Confederate

officer handed him an envelope, then climbed back up, and the ladder was withdrawn.

Andrews broke the wax seal and stepped to the window to read the paper.

His men watched him in silent apprehension. Andrews's lips compressed. Carrick and the raiders exchanged hasty glances. The rest of the prisoners in the hole stopped talking.

Without a word, Andrews handed the paper to Carrick. The other four crowded around to read over his shoulder. Carrick ran his eyes quickly down the paper, scanning the legal language detailing the charges of spying and treason, then the guilty verdict. His gaze halted near the bottom on the line . . . **and then and there be hanged until he is dead! dead! dead!**

Chapter Nineteen
Fuller's Challenge

Amelia Waymier awoke to the sound of distant thunder. She rolled over with a groan, stiff and aching from sleeping on the thin mat over the hard, wooden floor. She lay on her back, staring at the iron latticework ceiling of her cage. Her imprisonment had so far lasted only two and a half weeks, but already it seemed like months. Even though it wasn't important, she wished she'd kept track of the days. It must be about the end of April, or the first of May.

Hearing the thunder again, she thought a spring storm was coming. Good. At least it would cool things down. She didn't know how the men in the hole below were able to stand it. She prayed for them daily, especially for her son Josiah. Andrews, Knight, and Ross had been put down there, too. Maybe their presence would help bolster morale.

She sat up, feeling hot and sticky. She was more fortunate than the others, she reflected, running her hands over the clean frock she wore. It was a gift from Mrs. Swims, the jailer's wife, who had taken pity on Amelia's ragged, muddy state. She had also provided an old, threadbare wool jacket for her to use as a pillow, or to pad the hard floor. What Amelia really missed was a bath and the opportunity to brush her teeth. She wrapped a piece of the thin cotton dress tail around her forefinger and rubbed the surfaces of her teeth to make them feel a little cleaner. She had not bathed in weeks, and even though she had asked Mrs. Swims about it, the old lady simply said there were no provisions for prisoners to bathe, and she didn't know how long they would be in jail. From Mrs. Swims's comments, Amelia deduced that she would have no need of a toothbrush or a bath for much longer. A cold chill had gone up her back at the inference they were all to be executed.

She climbed to her feet and went to one side of the cage, straining to see out the window on the far side of the room. Where was old man Swims? It was early, but he was usually here by now. She had no appetite for the coarse cornbread and sowbelly he served twice a day, but she was thirsty.

The concussion of distant thunder came again, and it suddenly occurred to her that what she heard might not be a storm. The regularity of it seemed odd. That was the boom of cannon!

Hardly had this thought crossed her mind than the door from the outside stairway burst open, and Swims rushed in, panting and red-faced, his white hair flying. He snatched his ring of keys from a hook on the wall, hurried to her cage, and with trembling hands began unlocking the door.

"Where are we going?" she asked apprehensively, remembering his wife's words from the day before.

He didn't answer, but six uniformed guards came through the door with muskets and fixed bayonets.

Swims yanked her out into the room by one arm. "Stand there!" he ordered as he knelt and inserted his other key into a hole in the floor. He threw back the door and grabbed the ladder, sliding it down the hole. "Everybody up outta there!" he yelled.

Amelia heard a stirring down below. The prisoners had

obviously been expecting breakfast — not this. One by one they filed up, blinking in the light. She stood back, horrified by their appearance, and especially that of Carrick and Josiah — haggard, dirty, pale, unshaven.

"Form up in a line, right here!" the sergeant of the guard said. "You, too, lady!" he snapped, when Amelia didn't move.

"What's going on?" Carrick asked.

"General Mitchell's attacking Chattanooga," one of the guards replied as they herded prisoners out the door and down the wooden stairway. Amelia brought up the rear with Josiah and Carrick. Some of the prisoners were almost too weak to walk, and all were nearly blind in the bright daylight. The stronger helped the weaker as they marched several blocks down the street.

"Thank da Lord for fresh air!" Alex gasped, breathing deeply.

"Better thank General Mitchell, too," Wolford said.

The hollow booming seemed no closer, but, as they turned the corner, it appeared to come from across the river. Men and women were running in confusion, scattering before the artillery barrage. Now and then, Amelia saw the top of a building explode in a shower of bricks and mortar. Horse-drawn caissons rattled through the streets, and she could see soldiers marching in ranks a few blocks away. The Union forces had caught Chattanooga by surprise.

The two dozen prisoners reached the railroad depot. Several of the weakest collapsed on the platform.

"Sounds like we're saved, at long last!" Wolford cried jubilantly.

"I wouldn't get my hopes up," Carrick said. "Looks like they're getting us out of town before the Federals can liberate the jails."

A half hour later they were pushed aboard a passenger train, chains clanking, as they made their way into a coach and sat down. Amelia was thankful she wasn't chained. The few amenities she enjoyed as a woman would be of little help if their lot were to be hanged.

A few minutes later, the train started with a jerk, and they rolled out of Chattanooga, southbound, deeper into the Confederacy. Her heart sank, but she focused on the welcome sight of green trees, deep blue sky, and clouds. She tried to talk to her son and Carrick who sat opposite, but the guards were apparently nervous and under strict orders to keep the prisoners from conversing.

Every few miles their train was shunted onto a siding to allow other, northbound rail traffic to pass.

"There's a bridge we should have burned," Carrick said in an undertone, the regret apparent in his voice, as the train rolled over Chickamauga Creek.

"We sure missed our chances," Josiah agreed.

If Andrews heard the comments, he made no sign.

"Quiet there, you two!" Amelia jerked back as the guard stabbed his bayonet across the seat in front of her to emphasize his command.

At Cartersville, they were taken off for a latrine break and given a drink of water.

Word had apparently been telegraphed ahead that the train thieves were on their way south, for they were greeted at every stop by a throng of curious and abusive citizens.

Soldiers formed a line with their muskets at port arms as the prisoners lined up to use the privy outside the Cartersville depot.

"You'd think we were two-headed unicorns!" Wolford marveled as the crowd shoved closer, gawking at the prisoners who filed back through the depot to the train.

"Hey, you've had a turn. Get outta the way so I can have a look. I ain't never seen a real, live Yankee before!" A young man, dressed like a laborer, muscled his way to the front, then was restrained by an armed guard.

"You're likely to see a damned sight more of us than you ever wanted to before this is over," Wolford shot back.

Several of the prisoners laughed, and that seemed to infuriate the bolder men in the crowd.

"What the devil's that woman doing with them?" one shouted.

"She's the one what stole all that gold from the mint!" another yelled back. "Snatched it right out from under the guards."

"Whip her like a thievin', nigger bitch!"

"I'd like to do it myself," a familiar voice said.

Startled, Amelia looked up and spotted the balding head and accusing eyes of the speaker. It was none other than Barney Leathers, the keeper of the Cass wood and water station who'd helped pull her mules and wagon out of the mud at the end of that fearful night. He held her with a hard stare. "Hello, again, Amelia . . . or is it Jane Segal? You sure made a fool of me," he declared. "You can bet I'll be standing below the scaffold when they stretch your neck, along with all your Yankee friends."

She swallowed and averted her eyes as she shuffled past. She really had nothing to be ashamed of, she thought. Deception in war was common and expected, but her conscience, formed by her own standards of honesty, would not excuse her so easily. Lying was not something she could ever get used to. She began to have serious doubts that everything was destined to happen in a certain pattern. Randomness seemed the order of the day.

"How do ya reckon she got that gold away from them

three guards?" a man yelled.

"Whoa! That gal must be a hellion!" a fat, gap-toothed man observed.

"Yeah. She ain't too old for you, Zack. How'd you like to get astraddle o' her and go a few jumps?"

Amelia heard a smack like someone hitting a ripe tomato, and suddenly her son was on the floor, smashing his manacled hands into the face of the beefy heckler. Blood from the man's nose splattered his shirt front.

The hair-trigger crowd needed no more of an excuse to jump Josiah. Only the crush of bodies prevented them from getting free swings at him before the guards waded in, jabbing with bayonets and cracking skulls with musket butts. The crowd fell back.

The guards dragged Josiah away from the cursing man and threw him back in line, blood trickling from a gash on his forehead.

Amelia cringed. She had withstood invective before when she lived in Dahlonega, but that was nothing compared to the hate she could feel emanating from this hostile mob.

"Lemme see! Lemme see!"

"There ain't nothin' to see," the man being jostled yelled back, his hat falling off. "It's all over. Them Yanks look just like everyone else, 'ceptin' they're wearin' chains."

Cursing and sweating, the guards forced a path through the near riot to the door of the coach. Once they were seated and the train began to move, Amelia breathed a sigh of relief.

Nearly every stop along the way was the same, except that they were not allowed off and the mobs consisted only of faces at the coach windows. She was sitting on an aisle seat and tried to close her ears to the shouts and insults that were somewhat muffled by the closed windows.

At the Big Shanty stop, someone was sent to the hotel eatery to bring the prisoners some cornbread and bacon. It was the best-tasting food Amelia had eaten since she was captured, and she slowly savored her small portion. But the raiders, including Josiah, were not faring so well. They ate their food quickly, and stared out the windows, muttering that this was where it all began. From their aggrieved looks and whispered words, she knew the scene of the *General*'s capture was having a great affect on them. She was sure not one of them had ever thought to see this place again.

"Gawd Almighty, you peckerwoods smell like a damned outhouse!" the sergeant of the guard exclaimed. They'd been sitting in the closed car with the late-afternoon sun slanting through the windows. "Let's get some air in here."

He stepped between the seats and slid up the window; two other guards did the same on both sides of the coach. A breeze, scented with spring flowers and fresh earth drifted through the stuffy car.

There was no mob here — only a few curious onlookers, but Amelia was still glad when the train pulled out for Marietta. Here they stopped briefly, then rolled straight on to Atlanta. As the locomotive chugged into the depot, the crowd that greeted them was larger and more vicious than any they'd met.

"Shit!" the sergeant muttered. "I hope they sent a big escort." Before he could even get his men positioned, the door at one end of the coach was smashed open from the weight of bodies against it. The guards jumped to repel the angry mob, forcing them back outside and off the train.

Amelia was trembling, feeling helpless. True, she was

not chained as most of the others were, but the only thing standing between them and the furious mob were the gray-clad guards who probably had no more love for them than the Atlanta citizens outside their train windows. But, at least, the guards seemed determined to do their job and deliver the prisoners safely from train depot to city jail, however far away that might be. She was sure they'd probably have to walk; no transportation would be provided for them, unless they were to be incarcerated several miles away.

Carrick leaned out of the way as hands grabbed at them through the open windows.

Amelia happened to see a well-dressed man with side whiskers raise his cane and, with one quick motion, slip the handle off to reveal a slim, deadly sword hidden inside.

"Look out!" she screamed.

Carrick reacted instantly and slammed his chained hands down on the blade, deflecting it into the cushion of the seat back. "Arrest that man!" the sergeant of the guard yelled. The top-hatted man let go of his sword and ran, disappearing into the crowd on the platform.

A rock smashed the window, and Amelia ducked away from the slivers of glass that showered them.

Another hand came through the window, this one holding a folded newspaper. "A friend!" came a voice from below the edge of the window, and the paper was dropped. While the guards were distracted, Josiah snatched the paper and stuffed it inside his shirt.

"OK, boys, form up and be ready!" the sergeant ordered. "Let's get these Yanks out of here!"

The prisoners were herded to the end of the car. Then, flanked by the armed guards, the party forced its way through the jeering mob on the platform and started down the middle of the street in a column of twos. They shuffled along, chains rattling and dragging on the cobblestones, but the sound could barely be heard above the noise of the crowd that followed them, hurling insults.

"Damned Yankee scum!"

"Steal our trains, will ya? Hanging's too good for ya!"

"Take that, you Yankee nigger-lover!" The burly speaker lunged for Andrews, but the guard was quicker and clipped him on the jaw with the butt of his musket. The attacker dropped like a sack of sand, and the crowd surged over him.

"Never thought I'd be defendin' this bunch!" the guard grunted to the next one behind him.

"Yeah, but I ain't lettin' these loud-mouthed sons-o-bitches take *my* prisoners," the second guard said, shoving two men aside.

The prisoners arrived at the jail, four blocks from the depot, and were escorted inside. The door was slammed and barred. After a few minutes of final insults, the irate mob gave up and began dispersing.

The soldiers seemed all too glad to be rid of their charges.

The Atlanta jailers divided the prisoners into three groups in three cells, separating the raiders from the Tennesseans. Much to Amelia's surprise, she was confined with the men, but was glad to be back with her son and Carrick.

Drinking water was provided in buckets, but no food. Exhausted as they were from the unaccustomed exercise and strain of the trip, they all sought a spot on the floor and fell asleep as twilight faded through the barred, second-floor windows.

The next morning Amelia felt almost human again.

She'd learned to ignore her long-unwashed condition. But she was a model of hygiene compared to her cell mates.

The turnkey brought them the usual cornbread and fat-back for breakfast, but at least the meat didn't have maggots.

After the guard came to take away the food bucket, Josiah pulled out the newspaper that had been dropped through the train window. They all eagerly scanned the columns of print and were jubilant to see New Orleans had been captured by the Federals. There were also notes of prisoner exchanges from Libby Prison in Richmond. This raised their hopes even more, but Sergeant Ross remained glum, expecting the worst. "On the trip down here you saw how notorious we are," he said. "If the Confederate government exchanged us, they'd have to deal with a riot among their own people . . . probably in the whole state of Georgia."

Andrews nodded his agreement. "It'd be bad for morale. The authorities have to make an example of us . . . me especially, since I've already been handed my death sentence. They won't let you go without some severe punishment."

"Oh, Lord, look at this!" Josiah said, turning to the second page. He pointed to an article headed: **Train Thieves Caught**. The writer crowed that now all of the raiders had been taken within two weeks of the train theft and that they would no doubt receive their just punishment. The names listed were the correct names of their former companions — John Wollam, Sam Slavens, Mark Wood, William Pittenger, John Porter, and several others who made up the rest of the men taking part in the raid — with the exception of the two accidentally left behind in Marietta.

This disheartening news settled on them heavier than

their own miserable condition. In the silence that followed, they fell to picking lice off one another, more to have something to occupy the time than for any hope of ridding themselves of the vermin. That would require scrubbing in hot water with plenty of lye soap, but at least this jail had a clean wooden floor and plenty of light and air. It was a step in the right direction. Escape seemed more remote than ever, now that they were more than a hundred miles from Union lines.

That afternoon, the door to the cell-block opened, and a man was shown in. He paused, hat in hand, surveying the seven people through the bars. He carefully studied each face as if re-familiarizing himself with old friends unseen for a long time. Amelia was sure she didn't know this man. Although the top of his head was completely bald, he seemed rather young and wore a fashionable mustache and goatee.

The stranger stepped closer to the bars. "You must be Andrews," he said. "The description fits."

"I'm J. J. Andrews," the bearded leader acknowledged.

"I'm William Fuller, the conductor of the train you stole," the visitor said.

Everyone stared hard at Fuller.

"So you're the one who ruined our plan," Andrews said. "I'll have to hand it to you," he continued after a pause, "your persistence paid off."

"I just wanted to get a look at the man I chased all those miles," Fuller said. "And this is some o' your crew," he added disdainfully, scanning the rest of them. "You had a lot of nerve to do what you did. And you almost got away with it. I hear they've just caught the rest of your bunch and will send them to Knoxville for trial."

This didn't seem to require an answer, although Amelia

was surprised that they were being put on trial so quickly. That was not a good sign.

Fuller turned to Amelia. "And you . . . the robber of that gold shipment. That *really* surprises me."

He pulled a hand from his coat pocket and unfolded a white handkerchief, displaying some tiny grains of gold. "I found this in the cab of the *General* and was baffled at first. But then the news broke of your capture and the gold bar you had with the markings of the Dahlonega mint. The guards who stayed at your home came out with their story and it all fit." He smiled with only his mouth. "And here you are, seemingly poor. I believe you've hidden that treasure somewhere for your own future benefit."

"You think I would tell you, even if I knew?" she asked.

"Oh, you know, right enough. You put it aboard the train at the Ross Station wood yard. Barney Leathers turned in that government wagon and mule team you left there. But . . . the gold was not found along the right-of-way and was not on the boxcars you unhitched or on the *General* itself. You've managed to conceal it somewhere. I'm going to give you a chance to make a clean confession."

"Don't tell him anything, Mother," Josiah said sharply.

"Oh, this is your mother?" Fuller looked from one to the other. "Yes . . . yes, I can see the resemblance now. A handsome young man. Now, wouldn't it be better for both of you to go to your Maker with a clean conscience?"

In spite of herself, Amelia shuddered at the chill of his words. He was either trying to intimidate her, or he knew for a fact they would be hanged, just as Andrews was sentenced to be.

"All of you are bold, clever, and resourceful. But you've come to the end of the line. I'll give you three minutes to make up your minds to tell me . . . or the officer of the guard outside . . . where that gold is hidden. If you co-operate, I've secured a promise from General Ledbetter that you will not be dealt with as harshly as Mister Andrews. If not. . . ." He shrugged and pulled his watch from a vest pocket. "You may confer among yourselves. You have three minutes . . . starting now."

Chapter Twenty
sprung

As Fuller looked at his watch, Amelia caught Carrick's eye and gave a slight shake of her head. She had gone through too much for that gold. She was not about to tell this brash young conductor anything. If she had any idea of revealing its whereabouts, it would be to no less than a general officer, in front of a roomful of witnesses. But she had planned and schemed and struggled to make that dent in the Confederate treasury and, even though it was safely — maybe permanently — deposited on the bottom of a swift-flowing river, it was a secret she would keep, no matter what. She only hoped Fuller or some Rebel officer didn't separate the raiders and promise each a lighter sentence or special treatment to talk. Apparently each man had hidden or thrown away his precious bar before being captured. In spite of the newspaper article, she couldn't be sure that every one of them had been caught.

"Time's up!" Fuller said, snapping his watchcase closed. "You've made your decision. The gold may be scattered here and there, since two more of the bars were found near where two of your gang were caught. We'll find it with or without your help."

"I don't think so." Amelia smiled. She caught a warning

look from her son. "Josiah, they already know I took it. I've refused to say where it is. I don't care what they do to me."

"Don't be so sure your sex will save you from the hangman!" Fuller snapped, going out and slamming the door.

An hour later, an officer wearing a lieutenant's bars came into the cell, accompanied by two armed enlisted men and a minister carrying a Bible.

"Mister Andrews, it's time," the officer said gently.

Amelia saw the big man's face become ashen white above his beard, but he never lost his composure. He turned to the rest of them and shook each one by the hand in a warm, firm clasp. "It's been a real pleasure knowing and working with all of you," he said in a deep voice. "You know, I've always been curious about what's on the other side of the Jordan," he said thoughtfully. "Now it's my turn to find out. I hope to see all of you there someday."

He gave them a last look and a wan smile, then submitted his hands to the iron cuffs. They were snapped into place, and Amelia watched as Andrews was led out of the cell and through the outer door that closed solidly behind him.

The *bang* of the door ushered in an oppressive silence to the rest of the group. For two minutes no one spoke. Amelia felt tears welling up, then overflowing down her cheeks. A sob caught in her throat. She'd known this man only a short time, but she'd come to admire his courage and leadership. All of the raiders had followed him faithfully. As far as she could see, the failure of the endeavor was no fault of his. Whatever mistakes he had made, he was certainly paying for now. The fact that she might be next never entered her mind at that moment.

For the rest of the day she and the four remaining men

didn't discuss any of this. Each of them was consumed with individual thoughts or regrets. Their supper was brought, and they ate in silence.

Amelia had been asleep only briefly when she was awakened by a metallic jangling, the grating of a key in a lock, and the creaking of the cell door.

"C'mon! Up outta there," a rough voice said.

The windowpanes were black, and her first thought was they were all to be taken out and hanged during the night. A shielded lantern the jailer carried sent elongated shadows wavering and darting along the walls.

The men groaned and stirred. "Damned short night. What do you want?" Carrick asked.

"You're going back to Chattanooga. That shelling was a false alarm," the jailer answered. "And I'll sure be happy to get your lousy carcasses out of my jail."

"Couldn't this wait until morning?" Josiah grumbled, being the last and most difficult to waken.

The East Tennesseans were brought from their cells, and the entire group of more than twenty slipped quietly out into the night. To facilitate a silent march to the depot, the wrist and ankle chains were removed. The men rubbed their chaffed wrists, and swung their arms to stretch muscles.

"By God, that's a relief," one of the men said as his leg chains were unlocked. "Now I can take a full stride!" Weeping sores circled his ankles.

"Don't be tempted to stride too far," one of the armed guards warned him.

The shuffling walk through the dark streets of Atlanta was nearly silent. Amelia couldn't help but compare it to their riotous arrival along these same streets a short time before. She guessed it was about half past four in the morning. The iron-rimmed wheels of a milk wagon ground over the cobblestones, the *clopping* of the horse's hoofs echoing from the dark buildings along the street. The driver slouched, half asleep, on the seat. The only other person they passed was a drunk, slumped in a doorway.

In an ironic twist of fate, the *General* was hitched to the head of the train they climbed aboard. It was apparently back on its regular run to Chattanooga.

Once seated in the coach, Amelia dozed off, but was shortly jerked awake as the train made its Big Shanty breakfast stop. The unfettered prisoners were not allowed off, but the food brought aboard was the usual cornbread, molasses, and bacon. Amelia and several of the others savored the taste of something sweet, after so long without it. A big jug of coffee was even passed around.

By early afternoon they were back in Swims's jail, Amelia occupying the cage on the upper floor and the men again crowded into the stifling hole. Until everyone was locked in, Amelia held up well. Then the depressing fact of returning to this same terrible place overwhelmed her. She sat down in a corner and sobbed, clutching a double handful of the cotton dress to her face. Her misery was so deep she didn't even care if Swims witnessed her crying. After a glimmer of hope, provided by fresh air, exercise, slightly better food and quarters, being thrown back into this pigsty was the most depressing thing she'd ever experienced. Perhaps Andrews was now better off than they, she thought, as her body shook with sobs.

Finally she felt drained and ceased to cry. Drying her eyes, she realized she had to pull herself together. She could not afford to let her emotions take control of her. In any case, most of her tears had been for the men below, especially for her son.

Two hours later, just before supper, two armed guards came into the jail and Sergeant-Major Marion Ross was removed from the dungeon and led away.

"Where're they taking him?" Amelia asked.

Swims, who had been nipping at a flask from his desk most of the afternoon, was more garrulous than usual. "Sendin' him to Knoxville for trial with some o' the other train thieves," he replied.

"Why him?" she pressed, wondering if they somehow knew Ross had tried to wreck the *Texas*.

"Hell, lady, how should I know? General Ledbetter ain't in the habit o' consultin' me."

The authorities didn't know that Knight was the engineer, she thought, or he would have been taken as well. Before she could give this any more thought, the sound of singing came to her ears. The mellow tones of "Swing Low, Sweet Chariot" drifted up through the floor beneath her. She was astonished. The men in the hole were singing. She listened for a few moments, then found herself humming along. She supposed they were trying to keep up their spirits.

At first Swims seemed surprised, then amused, then he ignored the sound and went about his business. But the singing continued without let-up, from one song to another — "Go Down, Moses", "Tenting Tonight On the Old Camp Ground", "Bonnie Blue Flag", then the plaintive notes of "Barbara Allen".

Finally old Swims threw down his newspaper and jumped out of his chair. "Damnation! They all turned into songbirds! What the hell have they got to be so happy about?" He stomped out, and slammed the door.

The music may have been an irritant to the jailer, but Amelia found her mood uplifted by the songs. Whatever discordant notes the prisoners hit were softened by being filtered through the floor. To Amelia, it sounded as if she were being serenaded from outside the window.

Except for a break at supper, the entertainment continued until Swims locked up and went home for the night. Hardly had the jailer clumped down the outside stairs and departed, when the singing stopped.

A half hour later, as Amelia lay on her mat, she became aware of a scratching sound. She shivered, aware that they likely shared this old building with rats or mice. The sound continued — a regular scraping noise. Probably a rodent gnawing through something. She put it out of her mind, and drifted off to sleep.

The next morning the singing resumed. Swims opened the trap and hauled up their slop buckets, then sent down two buckets of water and their breakfast.

A half hour later, he grabbed the stick of wood he used to prop open a window and pounded on the floor. "Shut up down there!"

"Hail, Columbia" continued to filter up from below. "Amazing Grace" followed, and then the rousing strains of "John Brown's Body".

"Trying to drive me crazy," Swims muttered. "But they won't do it!"

By afternoon, Swims was nipping at the flask in his desk and taking more frequent walks outside into the encircling stockade.

Amelia dozed through the stifling heat of the late afternoon, lulled by the sounds of the music. At supper, she washed down the tasteless morsel of cornbread and flabby fatback Swims shoved through the bars. The singing had somehow restored her mental strength. It had to remain firm. After all, when planning her theft of the gold, she'd had a very positive premonition that everything was destined to work out in her favor. She must not lose faith now.

With that thought to bolster her, she spent the rest of the evening reliving scenes of her girlhood and youth — carefree years before the trials of adult life had beset her. She went to sleep relatively content that night. With the man's wool jacket rolled up for a pillow, she slept well in spite of the hard floor.

Late afternoon the following day, the door opened and a tall, uniformed Confederate officer strode into the room.

"You Swims?" he demanded.

Startled, the jailer dropped a hunk of cake on his desk, and brushed crumbs from the white stubble on his chin. "Yeah."

"I'm Lieutenant Allen Clark, here to take custody of those train thieves."

"Damn, Lieutenant," Swims whined. "Your men just brought 'em back two days ago. Wish you'd make up your mind. I'll have to hire a damned bookkeeper to figure out how much the government owes me for their keep."

"They're being shipped to Knoxville."

"Why didn't you take them when you took that Ross fella?"

"That's none of your concern. Just hand them over."

Swims grumbled something under his breath as he fumbled for his key ring. "I don't remember seeing you before."

"The Army moves around. I was just transferred in from Atlanta."

Amelia watched this with a sinking feeling in her stomach. Their trial was coming quickly. Could the scaffold be far behind?

"Hold it!" Lieutenant Clark said.

"What?"

"Let Amelia Waymier out first."

"You know her name?"

"We have a list of all the train thieves," he said, consulting a paper he pulled from his side pocket.

Swims selected another key, and came to the cage. He unlocked and swung the door open. Amelia stepped out to one side. She had a strange feeling about this man. What was different about him? Then she realized that his hair and mustache were gray. He seemed much too old to be a lieutenant. But then, in this war, things were not normal. Young men got fast battlefield promotions. Older men were given commissions through influence. This man was not in command of troops. Maybe he was relegated to escort or desk duty. Yet he had the presence of command. Confidence emanated from him. A holstered pistol was belted around his gray uniform coat, but there were no sentries with him. She eyed the officer. He seemed vaguely familiar. Had she seen him somewhere before?

Swims slid the ladder down the dark hole.

"Waymier, Knight, Carrick, Wilson!" the lieutenant called out.

The four men came up the ladder, blinking, into the morning light that flooded the room.

Swims backed up as if fearful of these unchained prisoners. "Where are the sentries?" he asked, glancing toward the door.

"Don't need them," Clark replied, pulling his revolver. He swung the barrel toward Swims. "Down you go."

The jailer's mouth fell open, and his eyes went wide.

"Not a sound or you're a dead man," Clark said quietly.

Amelia felt a thrill as she recognized him. This was the spy Andrews had introduced to them when they were delayed at Kingston!

Swims's prominent Adam's apple bobbed up and down as he swallowed. "You don't dare shoot, or the guards will be up here in two seconds," he said, a defiant light in his eyes. He opened his mouth. "HEL . . . !"

Before the shout was fairly out, Clark sprang at Swims, and the two of them crashed to the floor. Clark clamped a hand over the smaller man's mouth. Carrick jumped in to help. Josiah snatched the bandanna out of Swims's pocket and stuffed it into the jailer's mouth. A strip of cotton torn off Swims's shirt tail secured the gag in place.

"Let me get a couple o' licks at him!" one of the Tennesseans growled, as the rest of the men swarmed up out of the hole.

"Another time!" Clark shoved the man aside, and holstered his pistol. "Give me a hand," he said to Carrick. Clark snatched off Swims's galluses, and secured the jailer's wrists to his ankles. "That'll do it until we can get out of here," he said, giving the knot a final tug. Four of the men lifted Swims and slid him down the hole, using the ladder as a guide. He fell with a thump the last few feet. They yanked up the ladder and closed and locked the trap door. Clark threw the ring of keys into a far corner.

"Let's go!" Wolford said eagerly. "All of us can rush those guards at the gate. I got Swims's pistol out of his desk."

"No!" Clark said sharply. "We wouldn't have a chance. Besides, I came for these five. Give me a few minutes to bluff my way past the sentries at the gate. Then it'll be dark enough for the rest of you to have a chance to spread out and go over the back wall. There are guards posted at intervals around the yard, so you might want to create some kind of disturbance as a diversion."

"You can't stop us if we want to storm the gate," one man said defiantly.

"No, I can't. But it's suicide if you try."

"He's right," Wolford said thoughtfully. "Thanks for getting us this far, mister. Who are you, anyway?"

"A spy for the Union," Clark said, moving quickly to the window and drawing his revolver. "Are the five of you strong enough to run if we have to?"

"Yes," Carrick answered for them.

"At least, they haven't put chains on you. Act like you're my prisoners and don't say anything."

He went to the door and opened it a crack. "All right, let's go. Walk slowly ahead of me."

Knight, Wilson, Carrick, Josiah, and Amelia Waymier filed out and down the wooden stairway.

Amelia saw the sentries pacing at their posts here and there. Two had stopped to smoke and were leaning on their muskets, looking bored.

Six uniformed guards were milling around by the open gate, chatting, borrowing and lending chews of tobacco. One of them wearing sergeant's chevrons gave a half-hearted salute as the party approached. "Where you takin' these prisoners, Lieutenant?"

"General Ledbetter wants to question them about the disappearance of that gold shipment."

"At this hour?"

Clark shrugged. "The general is man of odd habits. I've known him to work all night and nap most of the day."

The sergeant had a pained look on his face that Amelia

could barely see in the gathering dusk. "The safeguarding of these prisoners is my responsibility," he said.

"It's mine and the general's as well. And when he gives me an order to bring them to headquarters, I deliver them."

"Yes, sir!" The sergeant saluted, and stepped back out of the way. "Corporal Stubblefield, take three men and assist the lieutenant in escorting these prisoners to the general's headquarters."

"Keep your men here, Sergeant," Clark said quickly. "I don't need them."

"They're not busy, sir. It'll be much safer."

"No need for an escort. I can handle this."

"Better not take the chance."

"Sergeant, do you have a problem with your hearing?" Clark snapped. "I said no escort. That's an order."

"Yes, sir. Sorry, sir." He came to attention and saluted as the gray-uniformed officer followed his charges out the gate at an easy walk down the street.

Amelia let out a long sigh of relief, then stretched out her stride to keep up with the men as they picked up their pace.

"Bear right at the next corner," Clark said quietly from behind them.

The party marched on into the darkness with no interference, and Clark, looking back over his shoulder every few minutes, directed them several blocks to the railroad depot.

To Amelia's recollection, the men had not taken time to tie Swims as securely as they might have. She could visualize the wiry little devil twisting and squirming out of his bonds already. Once he shouted a warning out the tiny window of the dungeon, the guards would be after them in minutes. But the other prisoners would probably make their break before then. Hardly had this thought passed through her mind when she heard the sound of distant musket fire somewhere behind them.

The platform of the depot was swarming with soldiers, porters, and civilian passengers. A group of men was busy unloading burlap bags from a freight car on a siding.

"A northbound passenger train is due in here within a quarter hour," Clark said. When they were grouped at one end of the platform, he holstered his pistol, propped one foot up on a barrel, and dusted off his polished boot. A casual observer would never have suspected the ragged, dirty group had any connection with this Confederate officer. "The train is headed for Knoxville, but we'll get off long before then," he continued as if talking to the floor. "The underground will hand you on from there."

He straightened up and consulted his watch, then gnawed at the corners of his sweeping mustache — the only outward sign of nervousness. If Amelia hadn't known better, she would've thought this tall, graying officer was late for some assigned military duty, irritated that his train was overdue. She watched his blue eyes under the hat brim as they darted here and there, taking in everything.

Josiah patted his mother's arm. "Everything's going to be all right as soon as we get away from town."

"What happened to your hands?" she asked, seeing the swollen, reddened hand on her arm.

"Didn't you hear us singing?" he asked. "My throat's raw, too."

"Yes, I heard you."

"We were sawing our way through the floor next to the trap door hinge, and the songs were to cover up the noise we made."

"How . . . ?"

"One of the men had a Case knife," Carrick explained

quickly. "We filed some notches in the blade to make a saw. Then we took turns standing on one another's shoulders to reach the ceiling.

"Once they took Ross, we figured we were going to be next, so we'd better try anything we could to get out of there," Josiah said. "It was mighty hard work, but this man, Clark, saved us."

"Maybe not yet," she said nervously. But when she looked at Clark, she had a sense of security. "Josiah, do you have a pocket comb?"

He fumbled in his pants pocket and pulled out a black comb. "Afraid it's not too clean," he said, wiping it on his shirt tail and handing it over.

She ran it through her wavy hair, clearing the snags and tangles. She wished she had a looking glass.

Several minutes dragged by before they heard a bell *clanging* and the northbound passenger train chugged into the station and screeched to a halt in a *hiss* of escaping steam. The train consisted of a locomotive and tender, three passenger coaches, a baggage car, and a caboose.

"I'll pay the conductor after we get on," Clark said under the clatter of detraining passengers and the banging of boxes being thrown off the baggage car.

Clark looked down the platform and suddenly stiffened. An officer led four armed soldiers toward them.

"Get aboard the train! Now!" he said urgently under his breath.

They obeyed without question, quickly climbing the steps of the last passenger coach and going inside as if they were ticketed riders.

Amelia slid into a seat next to an open window and carefully watched the scene only a few yards away.

A short, red-faced officer was confronting Clark, but she

couldn't catch the words over the clatter of freight and the shouts and laughter of passengers. A sudden lull in the racket allowed her to catch the words: ". . . General Ledbetter's headquarters . . . impersonating an officer . . . prisoners . . . papers. . . ."

Amelia strained to hear more, but failed. Clark had his back to her, so she was unable to hear his reply. Judging from his gestures, he was putting up an indignant defense.

The deep-throated steam whistle blasted a signal for their departure. The train jerked into motion.

"We've got to help him!" Amelia cried, springing from her seat and yanking open the back door.

"Mother, come inside!" Josiah said, grabbing her arm. "There's nothing we can do."

"He's right," Carrick agreed. "He got us out. Now we're on our own."

Knight and Wilson joined them on the back platform as the train began to roll.

"The alarm's out," Wilson said. "We'll have to get off before the next town that has a telegraph."

"There's a tank twenty miles ahead," Josiah said. "If I remember right, that's a regular water stop."

Amelia glued her eyes on Clark. The train was slowly gathering speed. Just as she leaned out to keep him in sight, he shoved the short officer into the men, then leaped from the platform and sprinted for the train.

"Oh, Lord!" Amelia gasped as two of the soldiers untangled themselves, raised their muskets, and fired. A lead ball smashed the window in the end door of the car, just above her head. The short officer rolled to his feet and yelled something at his men to stop firing.

But the train was rapidly drawing away from the depot, and Clark was losing ground as his hat flew off.

"Come on!" she screamed at him. "Run!"

"You can do it!" Carrick yelled, squeezing in beside her shoulder.

With a burst of speed worthy of a younger man, Clark lunged for the iron railing. Both hands caught it, but he lost his footing. The weight of his dragging legs jerked one hand loose, but several pairs of hands flashed out and grabbed Clark's arms, pulling him onto the steps.

"Thanks!" he managed to gasp, struggling to a sitting position. "Get inside. We've got . . . to get ready . . . for our next move."

Chapter Twenty-One
clark, the spy

The moonless night helped the party disappear into the darkness. They had abandoned the train at the water stop, twenty miles from Chattanooga, casually sauntering out opposite ends of the car, one and two at a time. To avoid attention from other passengers, the raiders gathered on the side away from the water tank and melted into the woods.

They were on the run again, but this time Amelia felt more confident of their success. They were following a man who knew the terrain and had a network of Union people in the area.

Clark led them silently, without hesitation, through a patch of woods and down a road between two fenced fields. Twice they saw lighted houses, and their passage roused some barking dogs. They alternated fast walking with short bursts of running for nearly two hours before halting in a wooded area for a much needed rest.

"How're you holding up?" Clark asked as they sat on the grass, breathing heavily.

"I'm tired," Amelia admitted.

Clark chuckled. "From what I've been reading about a certain Missus Amelia Waymier, you'll outlast us all."

She felt herself blushing and was glad he couldn't see it.

"Were those soldiers from the detachment at Swims's jail?" she asked to hide her embarrassment.

"No. The rest of the prisoners made their break shortly after we left. Some got away and some were captured, according to that captain. The guards released Swims, then two men were sent on the double to General Ledbetter's headquarters to find us. When they got there, the general ordered a patrol to the depot, guessing where we might have gone.

"He guessed right," Carrick said. "They almost had you."

"I wasn't a teacher of elocution for nothing," Clark said. "I *very nearly* convinced him that I was really a Confederate lieutenant and knew nothing about what happened at the jail." He shook his head. "But the main thing is . . . we got away."

"It was close," Amelia said.

"Thanks for pulling me aboard. I just about waited too long to make my move." He grinned wryly. "I'm not as fast as I used to be."

A teacher of elocution, Amelia thought. She found this intriguing. She'd wondered if perhaps his background had included some experience as an actor. Playing a rôle on stage would be valuable to his occupation as a spy. But spies, she guessed, were habitual liars. Who knew if he were really telling the truth now?

"Is Allen Clark your real name?" she asked on a sudden urge.

He hesitated. "It's close enough for me to answer instinctively to it."

Hardly a straight answer. She couldn't see his face in the dark, so felt deprived of part of her intuitive judgment. Evidently he was reluctant to divulge too much of himself, even to them.

"Let's go," he said, pushing up from the ground. "It's time to move."

"Where're we going?"

"To a friend's house. But we won't get there before daylight even if we walk at a pretty brisk pace."

The immediate prospect of freedom gave strength to Amelia's weary legs. One more night and one more step toward safety.

"Wait till they get to the end of the row," Clark whispered the next afternoon as he lay in the weeds next to the base of a large oak.

Amelia watched from several yards away as Clark and Josiah stalked the lunch basket that was on a flat rock near the tree. It belonged to a pair of Negroes who were cultivating a cornfield with a mule.

"Now!"

Josiah's hand slid the basket slowly off the rock, and they eased backward through the weeds with their prize.

"They'd probably share their food with us if we asked," Amelia said.

"No doubt," Clark said as they walked through the woods toward the Tennessee River he had indicated was only a mile away. "I've found darkies to be most generous when it comes to helping the Union cause. But this time we can't take the chance. There are six of us and we need it *all*. Besides, I don't want even the slaves to see us and be able to tell anyone else."

Twenty minutes later, in some big timber on a high bank overlooking the sparkling waters of the Tennessee River, they shared the cornbread, boiled pork, and sweet potatoes. Amelia's appetite, whetted by the fresh air and exercise, was sharper than it had been since before they were captured.

She noted that the second-hand frock was even looser on her than it had been in jail. With all this fasting and walking, she might well regain a semblance of the stunning figure she'd had as a young woman. There was some good in everything.

After eating, all she wanted to do was to lie down in the deep grass and drift off with the soft May breeze rustling the cottonwood leaves overhead.

"I'll keep watch for a few hours," Clark said. "All of you get some rest. We've got a long night ahead of us."

Amelia watched the men gratefully find places to stretch out — Knight, their blue-eyed engineer, short and stocky, with blond stubble on his face; Alf Wilson, fireman, lean and dark-haired, looking worn down from their ordeal; Carrick, steady, reliable; and Josiah, the son she was so proud of. As if knowing she was thinking of him, Josiah looked up, met her gaze, and gave a reassuring smile. "Is it too early for chiggers?" He grinned, rolling up his jacket for a pillow. "Let's hope they may want somebody with a little more meat to chew on," he added, lying down with a grateful sigh.

When the men were reclining, Amelia got up and approached Clark where he straddled a fallen tree, checking the loads in his revolver. His gray uniform was smudged with dirt, soot, and grass stain.

"Allen?"

He looked up, and she read fatigue in his puffy, bloodshot eyes. No longer the dapper officer she'd mistaken him for when he'd first entered Swims's jail.

"Realistically what are our chances of reaching Union lines on this river?" she asked. "The truth," she insisted when he opened his mouth to reply.

He smiled grimly. "The fact is . . . I don't know. The

original plan was to take you by train almost to Knoxville, then on east through a network of underground Union people who've been helping runaway slaves for years."

"Have you taken anyone down this river before?"

"Oh, yes." He nodded. "I lived in Chattanooga before the war. I know this river all too well."

"What do you mean?" she asked, taking a seat beside him on the log. The closest two men — Knight and Wilson — were already snoring softly in the grass a few yards away.

"The obvious problem is slipping a boat downriver through Chattanooga and past the Reb pickets at night. The most dangerous place in any war is in that space between two contending armies. There are always pickets and patrols out. But if we are careful . . . and lucky . . . we can manage that. The river's not actually blockaded as far as I know. What bothers me more is the river itself. Several miles beyond the town there's a chute between rock bluffs where the river narrows, then makes a hard left turn. I've known many experienced fishermen and boaters who were drowned there in years past."

"Can't we land before we get there?"

"Yes, but then we'd have all the hazards of land travel . . . rough terrain, scarcity of food, slow foot travel, the risk of encountering Reb patrols and hostile farmers who'd turn us in. The river is definitely the easiest and fastest way to reach Union lines in Alabama."

She nodded, thinking she'd rather face all the things he mentioned if she could be spared from challenging the cold, rushing river at night. The terrifying experience of swimming the much smaller Chickamauga Creek at flood was still fresh in her mind.

"I don't know if all of us can swim," she ventured.

"Probably won't matter much, because the current in

that chute would overpower a swimmer anyway. Besides, I hope swimming is the last thing we'll have to do . . . if we can get a decent boat."

She swallowed. He didn't even know what kind of boat they'd use.

"My contact who fed us this morning said the Reb patrols are confiscating any unsecured boats on the river."

"Why?"

"To keep men from fleeing the Confederate conscript. My contact told me of a boat big enough to hold us all, but the owner had it chained up. I. . . ." He paused, then shook his head and thrust his revolver back into its holster, hooking the flap over it.

"What'd you start to say?"

"Nothing."

"Look, you and I are of the same generation. I can handle the truth, whatever it may be."

He turned and gave her a searching look. "You're a strong woman. And you've got a fine-looking son over there. Both of you and the other four men are my responsibility. I'm a good boat handler. But the problem, as I see it, is to locate a pulling boat that will carry six people safely for many miles, especially through the kind of high water we'll have to run in the dark."

Feeling his blue eyes searching her face for a reaction, she was careful to show only enthusiasm. "We can do it," she said. "We haven't come all this far to fail. I have full confidence in you. Just tell me how I can help."

"You remind me of someone I used to know."

"Who's that?"

"My wife."

She wasn't prepared for this. "Where is she?" Amelia finally asked carefully.

"Typhus took her two years ago."

"I'm sorry."

"No need. She was a fine woman. I have good memories of our life together, even though we had our problems, like 'most everyone." He was silent, and looked away for a few seconds. "When the war started, I needed something to do besides teach . . . something to help the cause and to take me out of myself. So a friend, who's an undersecretary in the War Department, wangled a position for me as a secret operative, even though I was over-age. But, except for a touch of rheumatism in the winter, I'm as sound as a Yankee dollar. That had something to do with convincing them I could do the job." He looked back at her and grinned, crow's feet crinkling the corners of his eyes. "Besides, who's going to be suspicious of an elegant-looking, gray-haired gent, dressed in a Confederate officer's uniform and carrying the right papers?"

"Allen, you don't have to make light of it to me. I've already seen how dangerous it is," she replied. "Who sent you to get us out?"

"My orders came through General Mitchell from the Secretary of War. The chase and capture of that train has been in all the papers, and the whole country is thrilled with the audacity of it. You're famous. My bosses decided they couldn't let you languish in jail and be hanged a few at a time. I'm just sorry I didn't get there in time to save Andrews and the other seven."

"Do you have any children?" she asked, suddenly changing the subject. She wanted to take advantage of his reflective mood and find out what she could of his personal life.

"One daughter who's married and lives in Indiana."

"I have one other son, besides Josiah."

"I know. I got the background on all of you. Your late husband was director of the Dahlonega mint a few years ago."

She nodded. "Wish I knew what I'm going to do now. Ah, well, one problem at a time." She smiled as she stood up and stretched. "Now for some sleep. Thank you, Allen, for everything." She leaned forward and kissed him on the cheek. A look of understanding passed between them, as only two people who've seen much and traveled far can know.

Chapter Twenty-Two
the river — a last hope

The lingering light from the evening sky turned the flat water the color of sliding quicksilver as the fleeing party swung the rowboat out into the current. The craft was barely sixteen feet long, Amelia estimated as she sat in the stern, nervously gripping the thwart. She was doing her best to ignore an irrational panic that lay just below the surface as the distance from the shore began to widen.

"Move back a little, Wilson," Clark said, pulling one oar to turn their bow downstream. "We need to even up the weight. Careful! Don't stand up. Move slowly. There's not much freeboard."

An understatement, Amelia thought. The gunwale of the boat rode only a few inches above the whirlpools and eddies on the surface of the river.

They had located the boat with no problem, chained to a tree on the riverbank. "It's not much," Clark'd remarked, eyeing the old boat. "But I doubt we'll find anything better available for miles. We'll have to keep an eye out for anything bigger and better and snatch it if we get the chance."

It had taken only twenty minutes to find a stout branch and use it as a lever to twist off the rusty padlock. They'd scrambled in and shoved off. Clark — the only boatman among them — was at the oars.

"War has cleared the river of commercial traffic," Clark told them, "so we don't have to worry about encountering any steamboats. Just be on the look-out for Reb patrol boats. They'll be showing some kind of a light."

Spring run-off had swollen the Tennessee to a mightier river than normal. Amelia saw where it had overflowed low-lying stretches of shoreline. The massive volume of water was sliding inexorably downstream at a good five or six miles an hour.

Sometime later her head drooped, and she dozed, lulled by the moonless dark, the silence, the gentle motion. The boat struck something, and she was nearly thrown from her seat. Heart suddenly racing, she flailed wildly for a hand hold to keep from falling. The men lurched into each other as the boat came to a jolting stop.

Clark probed with an oar over the side. "Run aground on a sandbar," he grunted. "Probably the head of an island." He carefully stepped out into knee-deep water. With two mighty shoves, he got them afloat again, then splashed back aboard. "Can't see a damned thing," he muttered, taking up the oars to pull. "Not even any stars tonight. Must be overcast."

Amelia was glad she couldn't see anything. She could almost imagine she was safe, that the hungry river was not sucking alongside their boat, only a few inches below where she sat.

Later in the night she was brought fully alert by the men's voices. She opened her eyes to see yellow spots of light showing here and there on the left bank.

"Keep still, men," Clark cautioned. "Voices carry over water. It's Chattanooga. If we can stay in the channel, we'll slip by with no trouble."

The party watched silently as the points of light glided past them. The water gurgled as Clark corrected their heading, pulling them farther from the shore.

A half hour later Amelia noticed dim lights, indicating they'd drifted dangerously close to the opposite shore.

"Allen, the bank," she whispered, pointing.

He jerked his head around from watching Chattanooga. With an oath, he began stroking with one oar to turn them. "Moccasin Bend," he grunted. "Troops stationed on the flat ground just above us."

Hardly had the words left his mouth when a voice challenged: "Hold that boat right there. Identify yourself!"

"Take it easy, soldier," Clark called out instantly. "Just a poor man trying to get some fish for breakfast."

"Bring that boat ashore and let me see," the sentry ordered.

Clark pulled hard and steadily on the oars, forcing the heavy boat toward the middle of the river.

"I said stop and show yourselves!" the guard shouted.

Amelia could hear scuffling on the bank behind them.

Clark was panting now, his oars ripping desperately at the water.

"Halt!" the guard shouted again.

Facing forward, Amelia wondered if the lights from town had silhouetted them on the water.

A musket cracked. She yanked her hand away, flinching, as splinters from the gunwale stabbed her wrist. Hunching over to make herself a smaller target, she heard the blast of another shot.

Clark never slowed his rowing as the men instinctively ducked. The excited voices on the shore behind them gradually began to recede. By the time another shot came, they were out of effective range, even if there had been light enough to see.

"Stay quiet and stay down," Clark panted softly as he rested on his oars. "We should be out of danger soon."

The few lights winked out one by one as the bend hid them. Another five miles and they were again drifting in what appeared to be complete wilderness. Amelia realized she could now see the dim shoreline. Dawn was sliding up, paling the sky. She didn't know how many miles they'd come, but each mile they sat in this boat was a mile she didn't have to struggle through woods and over rocks and up mountains. Whatever the dangers of river travel, they were infinitely preferable to traveling overland on foot.

Clark soon located a towhead on a long, narrow island and pulled them ashore. The men dragged the boat up into the thick willows so it was well hidden, and they settled down for the day.

The men allowed Amelia the privacy of the sandbar to bathe. In the semidarkness she stripped off all her clothing and bathed in the chill, shallow water, scrubbing vigorously with handfuls of soft sand until her skin tingled. She came out at last, dripping and shivering, but refreshed. When she'd dressed and returned to the boat, she met the men straggling back from having bathed at the other end of the short island.

They had only river water to drink. Sleep would make them oblivious to hunger for a few more hours.

Later that day Clark said: "We'll start earlier tonight. I want to reach The Suck before dark."

They looked their curiosity at him.

"It's a narrow stretch about ten miles from here where

the current is fierce. I want to be able to see when we go through."

"Can't we portage around?" Knight asked, rubbing a hand over his blond stubble.

"No. Once we're between those rock bluffs, there's no place to land. And if we did go ashore, we'd have to abandon the boat and travel the rest of the way afoot. As weak as we're all getting from lack of food, it would be next to impossible to hike those mountains."

Amelia had been forewarned about this, but still felt her stomach tense at his words.

"Just do as I say. Obey instantly without question, and we'll make it. We might get a little wet, but if we get through, it should be clear sailing to Bridgeport, Alabama and the Union lines."

"*If* we get through?" Carrick asked, arching his eyebrows. "Is there a good chance we won't?"

"Our boat is overloaded, and I'd be lying if I told you there's no danger," Clark replied. "But, with my skill, your co-operation, and little luck, we'll make it."

"A few prayers wouldn't hurt, either," Amelia said.

"Amen to that," Clark answered.

As the men parted the willows and shoved the boat back toward the water, Amelia was surprised at the perfect calm that came over her. She had unconsciously resigned herself to the will of God. If they were destined to die, they would die. If they were destined to live, they would live. It was all pre-ordained, and nothing any of them could do would change the outcome. Prayer was not for survival. Prayer was to tell the Creator that she was in perfect compliance with whatever He had planned for them.

They heard it before they saw it — an ominous roar

echoing from the rock walls of the enclosing bluffs. Clark turned around on the thwart to row facing the bow. With a pull here and a push there he kept them heading downstream, and Amelia felt the boat being pulled faster into the narrow channel. Layers of limestone formed sheer bluffs that rose several hundred feet above. Looking straight up, she could see the tops crowned with heavy timber. Even if any cabins had been in sight, the boat was now at the mercy of the current and beyond any human help. They were on their own. The early evening twilight was dimmed by the narrow cañon, giving the rushing water a gray-green hue.

"All right, here we go!" Clark cried above the roar echoing from the cañon walls. "Get a grip on something. Keep your weight low and balanced." He pushed hard on the starboard oar to force them closer to the left wall. "If we go over, hang onto the boat, and don't let go, whatever happens!" His last words were nearly lost in the rushing roar.

Amelia got onto her knees in the stern, and gripped the gunwale. She felt Josiah's fingers close on her forearm and gave him a quick smile. The boat shot past the rock face with dizzying speed. Amelia had a fleeting recollection of the speed of the *General.*

Suddenly Clark was pushing hard on one oar, trying to turn them. Peering ahead through the flying spray, she saw the surging current had deflected from an angle in the wall to form a huge whirlpool. They were moving too fast to avoid it. Amelia sucked in a quick breath. She was thrown across the thwart as a huge, drifting log slammed into the boat from the port side. The heavy boat spun sideways like a floating wood chip, caught by the outer edge of the giant whirlpool, swinging around. Clark was pushing at the oars, nearly lunging to his feet with the effort, as he forced them, stern first, out of the grip of the vortex.

When Amelia looked up, she saw they were out of one danger and into another. The boat shot up onto a ridge of water that had gathered itself in the middle of the river. Thirty yards farther, this ridge hit against the bluff where the river turned hard left. The ridge of solid green water was thrown back in a foaming mass, swirling, churning, as it sought another direction.

Clark shouted something that was drowned in the roar. Amelia felt the stern rising up under her — they were going over. The boat flipped, jerking itself from her grasp as she was pitched headfirst. For several seconds there was only an ice-cold, peaceful silence. Then her head shot to the surface, and she blew water out of her nose, gratefully sucking air. Flailing to grab hold of something — anything — she was conscious of being lifted up and down in the powerful surge. Through the stinging spray, she saw heads alongside the overturned boat a few feet away, carried along with her in the rolling current. At first she didn't have to swim to stay afloat, but still struggled toward the wooden boat as a lifesaver. The upturned boat was drifting too fast for her to reach it.

"Stay together!" She heard Clark's shout dimly, as from a long way off.

The weight of the saturated wool coat was pulling her down. A terrible fear flashed through her mind. Had she come all this way, endured so much, only to drown in this raging river? *Please, God, no!* she silently screamed. Stroking and kicking, she struggled to keep her head up to breathe. But it was a losing battle. She had to shed the coat. Her mind suddenly became very clear, and her panic subsided long enough for her to take a deep breath and let herself sink below the surface. The unbuttoned coat was too large, so it took only a few seconds of twisting to shrug out of it.

Freed of the weight, she kicked upward, the full dress restricting her legs. She stroked automatically to keep her head above water — to continue inhaling life-giving air as the surging water propelled them another half mile downstream. Now and then she saw a head bob up in the rolling current. The overturned boat was several yards away.

To her amazement, she was still afloat when the rock bluffs gradually lowered and the river began to widen. The roar subsided and the current slowed. She managed to swim a few strokes and finally got a hand on the boat as the men, swimming on both sides, pushed it toward the shore.

Ten minutes later they beached the boat on a sandbar and dragged themselves on hands and knees up and away from the river.

Knight and Wilson were coughing up water. There was no other sound for a minute except their heavy breathing and the deceptively peaceful swishing of the nearby water.

"Mother! Are you all right?" She felt Josiah pulling at her shoulders.

"I'm fine." She tried to smile up at him as she put a hand to his face. He hugged her close, burying his face in her neck. Then he pulled her to her feet, and they stood silently for a few seconds. Twilight was slowly gathering its shadows about them.

Finally, with unspoken purpose, Knight, Wilson, and Carrick staggered to their feet and, together, heaved the boat upright on the sand. Josiah went to help. The oarlocks had held, but one of the oars was snapped in two.

"Allen, are we past the worst of it?" Amelia asked, shivering in the light breeze.

Clark smiled at her. "Easy going from here to Bridgeport," he answered, brushing back the hair that was plastered to his forehead. "And to celebrate, come daylight, we'll land, find a cabin or a hen house, and get something to eat."

There was a weak cheer from the men.

Amelia was hungry, chilled through, and began to shiver violently.

"Come here," Clark said, reaching and pulling her into his arms. He enfolded her tightly. In spite of their sopping clothes, she gradually relaxed and the shivering subsided.

For the first time in several weeks, Amelia allowed her mind to drift forward to the future. Although exhausted, wet, and cold, she finally felt free and safe once more. "What are your plans after the war?" she asked Clark.

"Haven't thought that far ahead," he admitted. "If I survive, I'll probably go back to teaching." He looked toward the men who were busy pulling off their soggy shoes and wringing out their shirts and coats. "Actually," Clark continued in a lower voice, "I'd like to see a little more of you. Where're you going to live since you gave up your place in Georgia?"

"Maybe Ohio for now. I could go back to Washington City where I'm from. But everything will be different there, I'm sure. I don't want any sad memories, so I may start fresh somewhere else."

"I want to keep in touch, and not just by letter," he said.

She pushed back a little, reluctant to move away from his embrace, and looked up at him. "Since you can handle a boat, I might have a job for you during summer vacation."

"Oh?"

"I have in mind a little salvage operation on Georgia's Oostanaula River. It will pay *very* well, if we get there first."

The curiosity on his face was the last thing she could discern in the fading light.

Epilogue

The Andrews raid continues to fascinate people a century and a half after it took place. During the 1920s, actor Buster Keaton made a silent movie, *The General,* loosely based on this episode. In 1956 Walt Disney released *The Great Locomotive Chase,* a considerably more accurate telling of the story, starring Fess Parker.

The locomotive itself was heavily damaged by General William T. Sherman's troops when they destroyed Atlanta in 1864. After the war, the *General* was rebuilt and put back into service for more than twenty years. It was also an honored guest at encampments, reunions, and even a World's Fair during the remainder of the 19th Century. Old adversaries came together for these events. Conductor William Fuller, Anthony Murphy, and Jeff Cain had their photographs taken in front of the venerable *General* with several surviving members of the Andrews raiding party.

In the early 1960s, during the Centennial years of the War Between the States, the *General* toured the United States under its own steam. It was retired to a museum in Kennesaw (formerly Big Shanty), Georgia for permanent display in 1972. The locomotive is housed in a building alongside the tracks where it was stolen 110 years earlier.

But this was only after it was involved in one more great controversy. The states of Tennessee and Georgia were locked in a legal battle over possession of the historic steam locomotive. The dispute was finally settled when the U.S. Supreme Court ruled in favor of Georgia.

Since 1981, the fully restored pursuit locomotive, *Texas*, has been on display in the Cyclorama Building of Atlanta's Grant Park.

In the late 1880s, the bodies of Andrews and the other seven men who'd been hanged were removed from unmarked Atlanta graves and re-interred in the National Cemetery in Chattanooga. All of the men, except for civilians J. J. Andrews and William Campbell, were from various Ohio volunteer infantry units. The state of Ohio authorized a white marble monument to be erected near their remains. The impressive seven-foot-high monument, topped with a miniature bronze model of the *General*, was dedicated in 1891.

After abandoning the *General*, the raiders went through a variety of hardships and triumphs. All of them were initially captured, a few at a time, in little more than a week. A few wandered in the woods for days, wet and hungry, pursued by manhunters and hounds before being captured.

They attempted jail breaks from both Chattanooga and Atlanta jails. These were only partially successful.

J. J. Andrews and Private Wollam escaped from Swims's jail but were recaptured two days later on an island in the Tennessee River. Two escapees, John Porter and John Wollam, stole a boat and managed to navigate the Tennessee to Corinth, Mississippi where they rejoined Union troops. Mark Wood and Alf Wilson escaped from Atlanta and spent several harrowing weeks rowing and floating south down the Chattahoochee River, finally negotiating

Florida swamps before reaching a ship of the U.S. naval blockade in the Gulf of Mexico. Two others got as far down the Tennessee River as Bridgeport, Alabama and were recaptured.

Hawkins and Porter, who overslept in a Marietta hotel and missed the raid, enlisted in the Confederate Army until they could find an opportunity to desert. But their identity was soon discovered, and they were jailed. Their cover story of being natives of Flemingsburg, Kentucky worked against them, since all the other captured raiders had said the same thing.

A newly created decoration — the Congressional Medal of Honor — was later awarded to several surviving members of the raiding party and posthumously to a few of the executed soldiers. Overall, eight raiders were hanged. Another eight raiders eventually escaped. Traveling at night, begging and pilfering food, hiding in caves, fighting off bloodhounds with rocks, and stealing boats, they finally reached safety. The remaining six were transferred to Richmond's Libby Prison where they were exchanged as prisoners of war in March, 1863, eleven months after their capture.

I have rearranged and combined details of these experiences to fit my own fictional protagonists, Amelia and Josiah Waymier, Gibson Carrick, and spy Allen Clark. More than a hundred gold and silver bars *were* cast at the Dahlonega mint after it was closed for coinage. These bars were shipped by wagon over muddy Georgia roads to a safe Confederate repository. To my knowledge, they were never stolen.

A Union spy in a Confederate officer's uniform actually showed up at the jail where the raiders were being held, but made no attempt to rescue them. Shortly after, this mysterious imposter was somehow found out and had to leap on a moving train at the depot to escape arrest.

With the exceptions of Sergeant-Major Marion Ross's escapade inside Tunnel Hill, and Amelia Waymier's theft of the bullion shipment, the major episodes of this story actually took place. For details of these events I have relied on the published accounts of several eyewitness participants who continued to write about their adventures for more than thirty years after the war.

About the Author

Tim Champlin, born John Michael Champlin in Fargo, North Dakota, was graduated from Middle Tennessee State University and earned a Master's degree from Peabody College in Nashville, Tennessee. Beginning his career as an author of the Western story with *Summer of the Sioux* in 1982, the American West represents for him "a huge, ever-changing block of space and time in which an individual had more freedom than the average person has today. For those brave, and sometimes desperate souls who ventured West looking for a better life, it must have been an exciting time to be alive." Champlin has achieved a notable stature in being able to capture that time in complex, often exciting, and historically accurate fictional narratives. He is the author of two series of Westerns novels, one concerned with Matt Tierney who comes of age in *Summer of the Sioux* and who begins his professional career as a reporter for the Chicago *Times-Herald* covering an expeditionary force venturing into the Big Horn country and the Yellowstone, and one with Jay McGraw, a callow youth who is plunged into outlawry at the beginning of *Colt Lightning*. There are six books in the Matt Tierney series and with *Deadly Season* a fifth featuring Jay McGraw. In *The Last Campaign*,

Champlin provides a compelling narrative of Geronimo's last days as a renegade leader. *Swift Thunder* is an exciting and compelling story of the Pony Express. *Wayfaring Strangers* is an extraordinary story of the California Gold Rush. In all of Champlin's stories there are always unconventional plot ingredients, striking historical details, vivid characterizations of the multitude of ethnic and cultural diversity found on the frontier, and narratives rich and original and surprising. His exuberant tapestries include lumber schooners sailing the West Coast, early-day wet-plate photography, daredevils who thrill crowds with gas balloons and the first parachutes, tong wars in San Francisco's Chinatown, Basque sheepherders, and the *Penitentes* of the Southwest, and are always highly entertaining. *White Lights Roar* is his next **Five Star Western**.